Bob Moats

I0567255

Mortuary
Murders

By Bob Moats

Mortuary Murders

For information and address:
Magic 1 Productions
P.O. Box 524, Fraser MI 48026-0524
Website: http://murdernovels.com
Cover by Bob Moats

Bob Moats

Other Jim Richards series books by Bob Moats

For a preview or to purchase a book, go to
http://murdernovels.com

3

What people are saying about the Murder novels by Bob Moats

"I went online this morning and read your book. I thought at first that I would only read a few pages, but got sucked into it and read all 11 chapters. You are a very good writer! I read quite a bit and often pick up "Airport" paperback mysteries to read on a plane. Most of them are dreadful, with obvious plots. Classmate Murders is a much better story than most."

Ray Zink, Entrepreneur, Minn.

"I got up to chapter ten of the Classmate Murders and decided then to buy the next two books." ... "Just finished your third book, the Dominatrix Murders. I thought it was the best one of the three, didn't want to put it down till I finished it. I looked forward to see how Penny would greet (Jim) every day after her show. Keep the books coming can't wait for the next one."

A. Norris, Retired Naval Corpsman

"Classmate Murders is well written and keeps the reader involved and wondering what will happen next throughout the book. Showgirl Murders keeps the reader involved throughout the story and keeps you guessing as to who the murderer is until very near the end."

G. Shurig, Kalamazoo

"If you like mysteries and action then don't miss reading this book..."

Jan Schneider, avid mystery/crime reader

"I finished the book last night, and really enjoyed it. I can only read a book that fast when it keeps my interest, so that should tell you a lot. I would recommend this book to others. I look forward to reading the next installment of the book."

M. K., retired Chrysler Admin.

"I haven't finished the book yet, when I enjoy a book, I take my time, but I want to buy the other two books. I compare your writing to a Mickey Spillane novel, and I like your style, very narrative. I'm amazed you don't have a publisher yet."

Michael Rasah, Professor of History

"Thanks for making me immortal, love the stories, your friend, Buck."

The real "Buck", George Carver

"Your books have been a joy to read. They keep me interested until the last page is turned. Keep up the good Work!

B. Scharmann, Rochester Hills, Michigan

Mortuary Murders

Bob, my brother, Bill, sent all seven of your Jim Richard's novels for me to read. I loved them. They were interesting and fast moving. You did good and I hope you write some more of them. I gave the books to my daughter and now she says she is hooked! I enjoy your books and I want to see more of them. It is hard to find books of this type.

Fred Scharmann, Avon, OH

Murder novels aren't my usual fare but this sweet, suspenseful and often humorous series draws you in and keeps you guessing to the end. I've read all eight (some of them twice) and hope to see more coming soon. I recommend following Jim Richards adventures but take care, murder seems to follow him!

Tia L Brink, Binghamton, New York

Extra special thanks to:

Thank you to all the people who purchased this book. I hope you enjoy it as much as I enjoyed writing it for my faithful readers.

The Jim Richards Family of Readers is listed in the back of the book.

Mortuary Murders by Bob Moats

Chapter 1

The funeral home was crowded with well-wishers. Abundant flowers surrounding the coffin gave the viewing room a sickly mixture of fragrances, as Penny sat on a chair while people huddled around her, expressing their condolences.

Buck was standing before the coffin looking down at the body of Jim Richards, looking like he was made of wax. He probably was, since the explosion of Jim's Crown Vic had thrown his body from the car, most of his face was damaged and Buck thought that the funeral people did a good job of filling in the missing pieces around his face. Buck couldn't believe his friend was gone. He turned away and went to sit next to Penny as she held up well for her loss.

The director of the home closed the coffin and the guests were allowed to take a little time to talk about the recently departed. Lynn and Deacon talked about the cases he helped the police with around Las Vegas, Trapper talked about how Jim and he first met, over murder of course. I suddenly realized I was in an enclosed place; I was claustrophobic and started to scream for help. The coffin suppressed my screams, no one heard me as they lowered the coffin into the ground.

I was still screaming while Penny was shaking me in our bed. Damn, I hated realistic dreams like that. I sat up in the bed as Penny stood next to me now; I was sweating profusely and shaking.

"What the hell were you dreaming about? That was worse than the time you dreamt you were going down on the cruise ship."

"Crap, it was worse. You know I'm claustrophobic, I was dreaming I was in my coffin, but still alive. Damn dreams anyway. You were there, mourning me and Buck was there along with our friends. After they closed the coffin, I guess I woke and found I was in the dark and in a closed box. I was screaming, but no one could hear me because of the coffin."

"A coffin? That's not good Jim, it's bad juu-juu to dream about a coffin."

"Bad juu-juu? Have you gone voodoo now? You know I just got back from being out in Area 51 and had to go to a funeral home to help take Mark Huston's body in. I was all over the funeral home including the embalming room where ME Joe Lang did the autopsy on Mark. I guess my mind put that experience together with me in the coffin. Not a good thing, okay, bad juu-juu."

Penny was laughing so I slapped her on the butt, causing her to jump on me and she made good juu-juu to me.

We went out to the kitchen about a half hour later and I did my morning toast ritual. The new toaster that we bought last month worked very well, I was happy with it. Penny made her oatmeal and I sat at the snack bar with my toast as our toy Yorkie, Willy, was eyeing my food. I broke off a piece and dropped it to him on the ground.

"So what do you have planned for today?" she asked me.

"I haven't the foggiest idea. I'm going into the office and just sit until someone comes in to hire me to solve their mystery. I'm not taking any cases about aliens or going to Area 51 again. One time was enough for me."

"Well, you can sit thinking about how you saved Las Vegas from total annihilation at the hands of a terrorist."

"The military said to keep that on a low key, but I guess I can revel in my thoughts."

Penny went out to get ready for work just as my cell phone rang and the caller ID said it was Deacon. "Hey, big guy, what's up?"

"I need you to settle a debate I'm having with Klein over in missing persons. If a body from a funeral home turns up missing does it go to missing persons, homicide or to robbery?"

I felt a very cold chill run up my spine; the dream crept back into my head at the mention of a body from a funeral home. Coincidence?

"Was the man murdered?" I asked hesitantly.

"No," Deacon said quickly.

"Well, that lets you out. The guy isn't alive so he's not a person, therefore he is a property now and his body was robbed from the funeral home. So I'd say Robbery Division should handle it."

"That's what I said, but everyone is passing the buck. Actually, the body wasn't stolen from a funeral home, he was taken from a mortuary that preps bodies for burial. A business I could never do."

"What did Lynn say about the buck passing?"

"She's not here; she's in LA to testify on a homicide we closed a year ago, it's coming to trial now. The machines of justice turn slowly."

"Well, keep me informed about your missing body. On second thought I don't want to know, it's grim to think someone would steal a body."

"Or he turned into a zombie and walked out," Deacon said with a laugh.

"Then you'd better hide. I'm going into my office to sulk and wait for crime to come to me. If you get bored you can stop by to visit."

"I'll think about it. Anything to get away from here before Weber finds me by myself. Talk later." He hung up and I put my phone back in my pocket and waited for Penny to go to work. If you can call it work, she sits and talks to people in front of TV cameras and has women do her hair and make-up. Four hours of sitting around, an easy life.

She came out, gathered her purse and briefcase, gave me a kiss on the nose, and said, "I may stop in to see you when I get done for the day. We can do lunch at Bistros."

"That's sounds good to me, be careful driving in." I didn't want to mention Deacon's call about the missing body from the mortuary so soon after my dream, she likes to put things together to make a big

10

deal out of it.

After she left, I gathered my equipment to go to the office. I put Willy in his travel bag as I was calling it now, I didn't think it was appropriate for me to carry a purse. We went out to the garage, got the Crown Vic out and drove over to my building. I waved to the guard at the back parking lot gate and put the car into my reserved space.

I entered the building, let Willy loose and went by Trapper's office, he wasn't in. I stopped at Buck's door, he wasn't in. I was wondering if anyone was working today. In the lobby I found Lacey busy reading a woman's magazine.

"We have no work to do today?"

She about jumped out of her skin when she heard me, I had that effect on her. She calmed herself and said, "No, it's boring so far. Trapper took Sam and her brother to Denver for his surgery yesterday and Buck is home sleeping because he had to fill in for a guard last night at the new dealership."

"So it's just you, Willy and me today, huh?"

"Afraid so, unless someone comes in."

"Well, anyone wanting me to chase aliens, send them away," I said and went to my private office.

I spent the morning exploring the internet on my computer finding information about dreams, coming up with a bunch of mumbo-jumbo, and finally closed the internet down. I sat back staring at the poster I had made of Penny in her bikini from a picture I took on our mystery cruise. She didn't mind that I put it on my wall, she looked good in it.

I heard the front door bell tinkle and waited to

see what was going on. Lacey came to my door and said, "You are needed."

I got up, went out, and found a very somber looking man in a black Brooks Brother's suit that must have cost him a week's salary. He was very straight-laced looking, pencil mustache, and his hair was slicked back, reminding me of a gangster from the old black and white movies. Adolphe Menjou, the "suave" and "debonair" star of Hollywood movies from the 20's to the 40's came to mind. He had that bearing.

"Hello, I'm Jim Richards, may I help you?"

"I hope so, the police officer who called about my missing body said you were the man for the job. His name was DeAngelo" he said clearly and with great pronunciation.

"Yes, Detective DeAngelo, we're friends. Please come to my office." As we went, I realized what he had said, about a missing body. I was getting chills again and asked him to sit when we entered the room.

"And you are?"

"I'm Thomas Hannigan. Mr. Richards, I hope you can be discreet about my problem, it looks bad for business to have a body come up missing."

"Just what is your business exactly?" I asked.

"I'm a mortician; I prep bodies for funeral homes and save them the trouble and expense of maintaining a mortuary in their funeral homes. It works well for me, but to have a body come up missing, this is not good for business."

"So you want me to find the body. Can't the police help you on that?"

"There would be inquiries and police snooping around my establishment. Besides the police can't figure who to send to handle the case, I told Officer DeAngelo to forget it, I would handle it myself. That's when he recommended you."

"It's Detective DeAngelo and I'll have to personally thank him."

Yeah, with a shot to the head.
**

Chapter 2

"So you do the gory work for the funeral homes so they don't have to?" I said.

"Basically, yes. I started my business when a friend whose funeral home I worked for to embalm and prep bodies for viewing and burial, was having to cut back on expenses. People want to bury their loved one cheaply now, many are opting for cremation in lieu of burial. So I thought about starting my own business of just preparing the bodies for funeral homes, cutting out the extra expense. I can charge a lot cheaper than they could to maintain a mortuary and doing the embalming. Yesterday a body was delivered to me and this morning it was gone. I panicked and called the police before thinking it out."

"So now you decided to hire a private detective to find the body?"

"Yes, since it was a crime of stealing a nonliving person, there was no real crime to involve the police if I didn't want to file a request. Your friend said you could do the job, so I'm here."

"I'm sure there must be laws about the proper disposal of bodies, aren't there? To involve the police."

"Yes, to dispose of a body, you can't just dump it. There are procedures for the burial of a body, but theft is not covered in the laws other than simple robbery. Which I'm not filing with the police. Hence, I come to you."

I was now part of LVMPD's attempt to pass the buck. I'd have to have a heart to heart with Deacon about this. I wasn't happy with taking on this case after my nightmare, it was too close and too annoying. But I never run from a challenge, so I said, "Well, Mr. Hannigan, if you agree to hire me, I'll take the case."

"Very good, do what you have to do for the return and I'll pay you promptly."

"Here's my rate card," I said as I hand the card to him, then said, "I'll also need some facts from you to start my investigation." I pushed my pad of paper and pencil towards him. "If you can write out all the information about where your business is located, the name and disposition of the body, funeral home that the body came from, and anything else you may think to help."

He took the pad and started to write. I glanced back to the poster of Penny to get my head back into more pleasant thoughts. He finished about five minutes later and I took the pad back.

"I can't guarantee speedy results, this is not television crime, this is real life, but I'll do what I can to hurry it along."

"I hope so; the body won't be very fresh after a day or two, unless the criminals put the body in cold storage. I'll be waiting for your call." He took out his wallet, pulled out five one hundred dollar bills and put them on my desk, "Here's your retainer as stated on your card, you can send me your final bill when finished."

He stood, held out his hand and I shook it. I guided him out to the lobby and we said our good-byes.

I turned to Lacey, "Now I'm chasing dead bodies for a mortuary. I think I'd rather have aliens."

I went back to my office and dialed Deacon. He came on and I said, "I do believe that you had something to do with convincing the mortician to hire a private investigator rather than involve the police, didn't you."

He was silent for a beat and then I heard him giggle, "Who me? Never, but you needed the work so I pushed him in your direction."

"Well, I'm going to have to call Weber and let him know you are on your own since Lynn's away and see if he has any good cases for you to take on."

"Weber is out of the office for the day now; he had to go to some big deal meeting with the police commissioner and the city council. Something about the President coming to Vegas and how the police are going to handle it. So you'll have to hold off on the call."

"Fine, but I won't forget this; I will get back at you. What do you know about the missing body?"

"Not much, we didn't go into detail about the report. The officers who responded to the call, turned it over to missing persons, who called robbery, who called me. For some reason everyone thinks I have nothing better to do."

"Well, you don't. What did the first officers on scene report?"

"Just that the mortician went in to this cold room to prep the body and found his drawer in the steel wall was empty. Someone took the body during the night, is all they could figure."

"Okay, I'm taking the case, reluctantly. I'll be calling you frequently to bug you about it. So be prepared."

He laughed and hung up. I sat back thinking about how I would proceed. I had to organize my thoughts more as I grew older. I hated to admit it but I used to be quick in the thought process, but lately I had to think twice about things. Damn I hate growing old.

Penny came in about ten minutes later. I really didn't want to mention my new case but she would know. She had this telepathy that could penetrate my mind. I just waited to see how long before she got it.

She came into my office, smiled and said, "Chasing dead bodies stolen from a mortuary now?" Damn, she was good.

"Lacey told you didn't she?"

She laughed and said, "Yes, and I see trouble in your future. You dream about being in a casket and then you get a case to find a missing body. Coincidence? I think not. Bad juu-juu."

"Will you quit with the juu-juu stuff, it is just coincidence that this came up. It happens."

"More so to you than others. So when are you going to start sniffing out the body?"

I stared at her for a moment, "Sniffing out the body, that's disgusting. The mortician said if the body is kept in a cold place it should be alright for a while. I have his info on the crime and I will do what needs to be to find the late person."

"Is this a man's or a woman's body?"

I was at a loss for that, I hadn't asked. Dumb. It could be important to know. "I didn't ask but I will when I go visit the mortuary. I'll form my opinion when I know."

"Just don't be fooling around if it's a woman."

"Hey I'm not into necrophilia, so don't even start that. You can be so disgusting at times."

She sat with her evil little grin and said, "I just like to cover all bases."

We left to go eat at Bistros Restaurant and I sat most the time thinking about my case. For some reason I had a foreboding feeling about it. Like I may actually end up in a coffin. Not a pleasant thought since I already felt the panic of being in one, from my dream.

"So where in the world are you at right now?" she asked.

I gave her a blank stare then realized what she meant, "I was thinking about the case. This is a simple robbery, I just have to find the stolen goods and return them. Just like finding stolen jewelry."

"Yes, but you can't go into a pawn shop to see if your body was pawned."

"True, but I'll know more when I go to the mortuary tomorrow."

"Why tomorrow, the day is still early and I have nothing better to do than go casket shopping," she said with a big grin.

"We could go today, I suppose, but do you think you can survive a mortuary? This is not a funeral home with pretty flowers and beautiful furnishings."

"I can take it if you can big boy."

We finished our meal, paid and went out to valet parking. Penny's car was brought up since we took that instead of my Crown Vic. I was feeling wary since I knew Buck had said in my dream that I was blown up in it. Funny how you know what other people think in a dream. I would get back to my car when I felt safe, time will tell. Maybe I could drive the mini-limo I got from the mob family in New York, but that would look pretentious.

We drove out Maryland Boulevard and into a strip of buildings looking like industrial offices. At the end of one building, we found the front of the Hannigan Mortuary. I parked in front and we got out. I went to the front corner of the building to look down the side to see how it was laid out. There was a large overhead door big enough to pull a small service truck in, probably for delivery of the bodies.

Penny and I went to the front entrance and in to find a small anteroom with a woman behind a desk. She smiled and asked if she could help us.

"Yes, I'm Jim Richards and this is my assistant, Penny. We are here to see Mr. Hannigan, about his missing person."

She perked up when I said that and picked up the phone. Penny leaned to me and whispered, "Your assistant?"

"I'm maintaining my professional decorum. Would it look good if I had my wife tagging after me?"

"Assistant. I'll give you assistant. Just wait until bedtime, then see if your assistant is too tired to fool around."

"Fine," I said quietly as a door opened off the side and Hannigan walked out.

"Mr. Richards, so good you can get on this so speedily." He looked to Penny and said, "Why is this Penny Wickens, your lovely wife and host of 'Vegas Alive'? So good that you share your husband's interest in crime fighting. I watch you often."

"Thank you Mr. Hannigan, you know I'm not just some assistant, I help my husband whenever I can. We are a team, aren't we Sweetie?"

"Yes dear, we are," I said with a cringe.
**

Chapter 3

Hannigan took us to his office where he removed a file folder from a nice wooden file cabinet. He handed it to me, "This is the file on the deceased, John Hall, who passed away two days ago. He underwent an autopsy at the request of the wife, to see what he died from. He was only fifty-one. Joe Lang, the medical examiner who performed the autopsy, said that he died from natural causes; they couldn't find anything wrong or in question. The body was released to Spenser Funeral Home and they had the body delivered here yesterday to have it prepped."

He led us back to a large room with many small doors in the wall, all holding bodies; I was a bit creeped out. He continued, "I was a bit backed up, so many deaths this week, so I put him in a drawer and would get to him this morning." He pulled one of the drawers and waved his hand showing the empty body tray.

I looked at the thin handle attached to the door; there could be no usable fingerprints there, beside it being handled by Hannigan. I looked at the metal tray that would have held the deceased; I looked closely at the metal to see if there were any smudges, but saw none. If Hannigan had let the police investigate, they may have pulled some prints. If Trapper was still around I could ask him to come in to dust the thing, he was experienced in that.

"I'm sure you checked all the drawers to be sure he wasn't moved."

"Oh yes, besides, I have only two others who help with the embalming and make-up, they say they hadn't moved him."

"Do you have any enemies, someone who would like to see you shut down?"

"No, there are two other mortuary services like mine; I was the first but imitators started moving in. It's a cut throat business." He smiled.

"You mean it's not a dying business." I joked, he looked at me with a strange expression.

"Yes, I've heard that many times."

"You'll have to excuse my husband, he just back from Area 51 where I think they scrambled his brain."

I gave her a look and she suppressed a snicker.

"Oh, I heard about your adventures in alien country. There were rumors about a virus attack on the city that you stopped. Is that true?"

"I'm not at liberty to say, according to the government."

"I understand, you just answered my question."

I had to change the subject. "How much do you know about the deceased? Anything that may lead to his demise?"

"I really know nothing. I just get the bodies in and push them out. I don't get involved in their personal histories. You probably can talk to the widow, although I haven't told her about the disappearance yet. I was hoping to resolve this before I had to tell her.

"Well, to get to the bottom of this I may have to, but I'll hold off on it until I exhaust all other avenues."

"Thank you. Do you have any other questions?"

"How many funeral homes do you service?" I asked.

"I have seven homes I do pre-burial work for and I'm in negotiation with two more for their inquiries about saving money by using my service. I have been in business here for four years and never lost one body, this is not good."

"Well, there's a difference between losing a body and having one stolen. So I wouldn't beat yourself up too badly."

"Thank you, Mr. Richards, I appreciate the thought."

"I don't have any more questions for now, I may be in touch again and I'll let you know my progress."

"Thank you Mr. Richards and it was a pleasure to meet you Miss Wickens," he said.

"That's Mrs. Wickens-Richards; I just use the singular Wickens for the show, too much trouble to change my image." She laughed.

We left the mortuary and I was reading over the file that Hannigan gave me as we sat in Penny's car. There were a number of things in it that I would have to check.

"So, where to now?" Penny asked. She insisted on driving now, I yielded, since the whole assistant thing, I wasn't pressing my luck.

"I think we should go visit the Spenser Funeral Home, maybe they have some answers. It's now just before two o'clock so they probably would still have business hours going." She asked for directions and I gave them to her.

We arrived and parked, going into the funeral home. The sight of the viewing room gave me the willies, I still had the memory in my brain of the room. Penny took my hand and said, "Be a brave little boy and I'll give you a lollipop to suck on."

"Can I have a breast instead?"

She gave me a dirty look and let my hand go. I was on my own now. A very strange looking woman came up to us and asked if she could help us.

"Yes, can we speak to Mr. Spenser?" I asked for the name from the file of the person who authorized the transfer to the mortuary. The woman smiled and said to follow her. She turned and led us to a room outside an office. On the Door was printed, 'Michael Spenser - Director'. She knocked and waited, there was no answer. She knocked again. Nothing. She smiled to us, opened the door and went in. A few seconds later, we heard a scream, which startled me, and then I went into the room followed by Penny.

We found the woman standing over the body of Spenser with his head on his desk and a knife covered in blood next to his head. I pulled my cell phone and dialed Deacon. He came on.

"Hey Deacon, you are in homicide correct?"

He was quiet then said, "You know I am, why do you ask?"

"I got a murder to report. Now you have to go to work."

I asked the woman to carefully vacate the room

to preserve the murder scene as we waited for Deacon to arrive. About ten minutes later, he walked into the room followed by the crime lab people and a couple uniforms. CSI started to do their work as Deacon questioned us and the woman who identified herself as Agnes Hawthorn, the assistant director of the funeral home.

"Miss Hawthorn, did you hear anything from the office to give you a hint of what may have happened?" Deacon asked her.

"No, I was told by Mr. Spenser to leave him alone for the afternoon, I don't question him. He had no visitors that I saw, I'm always aware of visitors. The home viewing times weren't open yet, so there was no one in the house. That I saw."

"Ok, please give your statement to this officer," he said as he pointed to the uniform and he took the woman to the chairs in the lobby to get the info.

He turned to me and Penny then asked, "You guys heard nothing?"

"Nope we just got here about five minutes before we found him."

Joe Lang came out of the office and said, "TOD was about an hour ago, his throat was slit from behind, the perp probably snuck up behind him and did the deed."

"Snuck up, is that a medical examiner term?" I asked.

"Richards, I hear you are looking for a dead body, can't go after live people now?" he shot back.

"Funny. I need to talk to you about that body; you did an autopsy on him, John Hall?"

"Oh yeah, the wife was hot to prove something killed him, I couldn't find any signs of foul play. Now he's missing, strange. Is that why you are here?"

"Yep, he was scheduled to be on view here after they embalmed him at the mortuary. His body was taken from there this morning some time."

"Maybe he turned into a zombie and walked out?" Lang laughed.

I looked to Deacon and asked, "Do you guys share your comic writers? No Joe, he had help, I just need to find the people who walked him out."

The assistant ME was guiding the body out on the gurney so we had to move. They went out and I asked Joe, "Did you know this guy? I ask since you knew the funeral director up by Area 51."

"Nope, didn't have the pleasure, I don't know all of these guys, just a couple. We get together around Halloween and dig up bodies to set up in front of the morgue."

Penny was standing by listening and then I heard her laugh saying to us, "You guys should go on TV, I'll ask my producer if he can arrange it," and then she walked away.

"I think she doesn't appreciate the male humor," Deacon said.

"You call us humorous? I think our show would suck," I said as I went after Penny.

She turned to me and asked, "Can you get a ride back with Deacon, I need to go rescue Willy from Lacey and go home to dip in the pool to wash off all this death."

"You said we were a team, now you're punking

out?"

"Better believe it hotshot. I'm out of here."

I yelled back to Deacon asking if he could drive me to my office. He waved and nodded his head, I turned to tell Penny but she was gone. My wife doesn't wait for the world to follow.

**

Chapter 4

Deacon was talking again to Miss Hawthorn as I stood with Joe Lang, "You said that the widow of my missing body was trying to prove he was done in and not by natural causes?"

"Yep, she insisted that her husband was fit and not prone to any ailments that would cause him to keel over and die."

"Where did he keel over?"

"As I understand, the husband was some big shot in the unions that govern the hotel workers. He was at the Flamingo Hotel for a meeting in a hospitality suite for the big shots that ran the union. He took a dive onto the serving table and landed in the chip dip. I had to clean him off, one dip to another." He laughed at his lousy joke and then said, "I took him in and the wife was right there wanting reasons for his demise. I found nothing out of the ordinary other than he drank a little too much, liver was in bad shape."

"Hotel workers union? I guess that would be a stressful job. Did you turn him over to Hannigan

Mortuary or did they come and get him?"

"Our recently deceased funeral director here sent a wagon for him and I guess he delivered the body."

"Thirty minutes or it's free," I said. Joe stared at me, I said never mind.

"You're right, our comedy show would suck," he said and went out to take the coroner's wagon back to the morgue.

I went to Deacon as he sat with Hawthorn. I stood watching her expressions, she reminded me of one of her departed guests. It seems like the undertakers I had experience with in the past all looked like death warmed over. This woman reminded me of a spinster school teacher of olden days. Her hair was in a bun, lace blouse and cuffs, black business style outfit and those clunky shoes that laced up the ankles. She had a pallor about her face that needed make-up, otherwise she wasn't bad looking.

"Miss Hawthorn, again, did your boss have any enemies?" Deacon asked.

"None that I knew of, he was a good man, kind and gentle. He cared for the mourners and their needs.

Yeah, he probably cared for their money too, I thought. My mother paid a small fortune to put my father in his crypt. The funeral home tried to talk her into all of the little extras that added up to big bucks. But my mother was satisfied and happy with the arrangements even if there was no viewing, just the interment into the crypt, but it still cost more than I wished she had paid. I had seen programs on television about the high cost of dying, so I didn't feel sorry if people were cutting back on expensive things like fancy wood coffins or what kind of fancy padding to put in the coffin. I insisted that I was going to be cremated quickly when I die and put in a coffee can with no ceremony other than my friends having a wake for me, with plenty of beer and chips.

I left them talking and went into a deathly quiet viewing room where there was a casket set up containing a rather waxy looking man. I wasn't going near the thing, I had this dislike of seeing people in their coffins. I refused to view my father that way. I wanted to remember him as he was alive, not prone in a box looking lifeless. I studied the way they had the room setup and then left quickly as Deacon was coming down the hallway towards me.

"Well, not much more we can do here until forensics comes up with something. I'd say this was a pro hit, the man was killed while sitting in his chair at his desk and didn't hear someone come up behind him and slit his throat. The killer left the knife, but I'm sure there will be no prints."

We were in front of the office where the murder occurred, CSI was finished with the room, so we went in. I walked to the back of the chair where the man was killed and looked around. "He could have come in through that door," I said pointing to a door just off the back of the desk. I went there and opened the door realizing there was still powder on the knob from when CSI had dusted. I wiped my hands on a curtain next to the door, framing the opening, and then stepped out into a hallway followed by Deacon.

We looked both ways in the hall and there were four other doors. I went to the closest and opened it. It was a storeroom of sorts, with vases on stands for flowers and wreath holders. I noticed there were no windows, so I closed the door as Deacon checked another room. They were all offices or sitting rooms. Only one room had windows to the outside. One door led to the lobby right by the entrance where the killer most likely came through.

I said, "He would have to know the layout to navigate the doors and hallways to get to Spenser's office. Either the killer was hired and given the info or the killer is someone who knew the deceased and is good at killing. Either way, you should look into unhappy clients of Spenser, ones who felt they were taken for a ride by the cost. One death in the family wouldn't be a problem for some people, so to kill the guy who over charged may be a cinch."

"You think it comes down to an unhappy customer?" Deacon asked.

"Nope but it's some place to start. You got any other ideas?"

"No, I'll put Williams on it, he likes to waste time going through files for leads," Deacon said with a laugh.

"When is Lynn coming back?" I asked.

"She called and said the trial is going on longer than she expected. Maybe until next week. I'm holding up the best I can after that month she spent out at the FBI academy."

"You know there are plenty of hookers out roaming the streets, to take care of your needs."

"Hell no, Lynn would kill me if she found out. She's dangerous with a gun," Deacon said with a laugh.

"Yep, women are like that. So, I'm wondering if this murder has anything to do with my missing body. I need to find out more about my stolen property's background. I think I'll go visit his wife, even though I told the mortician I would hold off but it has to be done. I'll call him and let him break it to the widow and then I'll make my attack."

We left the building, Deacon drove me to the office and I went in to see what was going on. Buck was now in his office looking a bit tired. "Burning the midnight oils for your guards now?"

"Yep, good employees are hard to find and as many as I have, about half of them are worthless. They call in sick or Mac and I catch a number of them goofing off or sleeping on the job," he said with a groan.

"Gee, sounds familiar."

"I never goofed off on the job, I may have slept occasionally but never goofed off," he defended.

"I'll leave it at that. Good luck with your team. I have to call a mortician about a body." I saluted him, went to my private office, and sat at the desk. I picked up the phone and dial Hannigan's number.

He came on after four rings, must be busy with bodies. "Mr. Hannigan, it's Jim Richards, I need to talk to you. Are you busy?"

"I can make time; do you have anything for me?"

"I'll explain all that when I get there. See you shortly." I hung up and went out to the lobby; Lacey was deep in paperwork. I said quietly, "Busy I see."

She screamed in surprise throwing some papers in the air. I jumped back waiting for her to throw something at me. "Do you have to keep doing that!" she yelled.

"Okay, from now on I'll call from the hallway letting you know I'm coming, all right?"

"If you don't I'll have a heart attack the next time. You are evil!"

"So I've been told by Penny numerous times. I just wanted to let you know I'm back but I'm leaving again. Any messages for me?"

"No, you can go and don't do that again."

I smiled and left the lobby, going out the back door to my car. I drove over to the Hannigan Mortuary and parked. The same woman who greeted Penny and me was at her desk and smiled when I came in.

"Mr. Hannigan is expecting you, go right in."

I thanked her and went to the door and in, going to the room where he worked on the bodies, to find Hannigan slumped over a body on a table. My heart skipped a couple beats and went to him quickly. I touched his arm and he jumped, he was alive.

"Mr. Richards, I was just listening to the body's insides for gas before I cut into him for the embalming. He's a little riper than most and gas can sometimes build up inside if the ME hasn't performed an autopsy. This body was one whose family refused an autopsy, so I have to be careful when I start inserting needles and removing organs. I can put him back in his cold drawer so we can talk." He pushed the table to the open drawer and slid the body over then pushed him into the opening. He closed the door with a slam, sending chills through me. He smiled and asked me to follow him.

**

Chapter 5

Trapper and Samantha had checked into the bed and breakfast on the outskirts of Denver, north of the city. They had taken Sam's brother, Phillip, to the clinic where he was going to have the surgery to reassign his sexual body from male to female. He was put happily into a private room that Sam had arranged for and they said their good-byes for the night.

"This is a nice place," Sam said as they settled into the quaint room of the century old gingerbread style house. Sam had gotten the name of the place through one of the pre-op transsexuals who worked for her in her hair salon front for her bookie operation in back.

Trapper dropped down on the bed, smiled and said, "At least the bed is new."

"You would notice that out of all the antiques surrounding us. Speaking of antiques, how are you feeling?" she laughed and opened her suitcase. "We are going out for a good meal at some nice restaurant to celebrate our being here. My treat."

"I'm not arguing. Where shall we go?"

"We can ask the nice lady who checked us in. Let's go, I'm hungry." She pulled him from the bed and they went back downstairs to the small desk in the tiny lobby. There was an elderly woman sitting behind the desk, she smiled as Sam and Trapper approached.

"Is your room agreeable?" she asked.

"It's prefect, Mrs. Walters. We would like to go out to eat at a nice restaurant. Can you recommend one?" Sam said.

"Of course, dear. There is a real nice one just down the street; you can even walk to it. It's called the North Denver Eatery. It's not real fancy, you don't need a tie, but it has great food and the price is right.

As they stood there, a young couple came down the stairs and they were arguing loudly. Trapper turn to protect Sam as they were starting to fight. Trapper grabbed the man and held him, "Hey cut it out! Now!"

The woman was standing still and then she popped the guy in the mouth with her fist. Trapper let him go and grabbed her as she squirmed and kicked out at her partner. "Come on guys, cut it out before I call the cops."

She stopped and was silent when the mention of cops came up. "He's a bastard!" she finally spoke. The man spit at her and said, "I should never have come here with you, you're a psycho bitch! I'm outta here!" He turned and went out the front door, slamming it hard. Trapper let the girl go and she stood looking shocked. Then she turned and went back up the stairs leaving the lobby in silence.

"Well, I'd say they were married," Trapper smiled.

"No they aren't, they are engaged but it looks like the engagement is over," Mrs. Walters said.

"Well, if they start again, just call the police quickly," Trapper said and took Sam's arm and led her to the door. They went down the front stoop and to the restaurant.

~~*~~

Hannigan and I went to an office next to the embalming room and we sat. "Now what do you have for me?"

"You knew Spenser of Spenser's Funeral Home?"

"Of course, we were acquainted through work, we never socialized. Why?"

"He's dead, killed about two hours ago in his office."

Hannigan looked shocked and stared at me, waiting for more.

"He had his throat cut from behind while he sat at his desk. I went to him about your missing body and we found him dead. The police have already been to the scene."

"I can't believe that, he was such a nice person. Does this have something to do with my body?"

"That's what I was wondering, anything you might know?"

"No, I just received the body, Spenser never

talked to me about it, and he had some young man bring the body here."

"Do you know the young man's name?"

"He introduced himself as Harry, no last name. I took the body and he left. That's all I know."

"Well, I have to talk to the wife to see if there's a connection. I have to find out more about his background so I can figure out why he was taken. There is a reason and I think I can find out by talking to the widow. Can you tell her about the body so I can talk to her?"

He sighed and said, "It was bound to come, if you don't mind we can go to her home and I'll talk, then let you. Is that alright with you?"

"Works for me, shall we go?"

He excused himself to change out of his work smock and then came back. We left and I said we could go in my car. He had the paper with her address and I followed his directions. We arrived in an upper scale neighborhood, mostly money people live there. I could tell that Hall must have had a good paying job with the union. I parked in the drive behind a new Cadillac and we went to the door.

Mrs. Hall was an attractive woman, medium height, thin, well built and had puffy blond hair. Built up on her head reminding me of the women from the Jersey Shores show. She stood and asked, "May I help you?"

"Mrs. Hall, I'm Thomas Hannigan, I'm the person who is preparing your husband for burial. This man is private detective Jim Richards. May we come in?

She gave us a wary eye; I pulled my ID and badge and showed her. She smiled and said to come in. She led us to a living room and asked us to sit.

Hannigan began, "Mrs. Hall, I'm sorry to tell you but someone broke into my mortuary and removed your husband's body. Mr. Richards has been hired to find him."

She sat in silence and just stared at Hannigan, like she didn't believe what he was saying.

I spoke up, "Mrs. Hall, you did come in contact with Michael Spenser of the Spenser Funeral Home when you arranged for the funeral, correct?"

She finally changed her facial expression and turned to me. "Yes I did speak to him. How was my husband's body stolen and why?"

"That's what I'm trying to find out. Mr. Spenser turned up dead today and I think it may have something to do with the disappearance of your husband's body. Can I ask you a few questions?"

"Mr. Spenser is dead? What is going on?"

"Again, that is what I'm trying to find out; may I ask you some questions?"

She composed herself and said I could.

"You wanted the autopsy to find more than just natural causes in your husband's death, why?"

"Because he was a healthy man and there were threats against him. I put the two together and they came out to murder. But the medical examiner said he could find nothing to prove he was. Natural causes possibly created by stress and a bad liver was the findings. I don't believe it but the ME was convinced. So my husband is now missing. This is getting very interesting."

"What was your husband's occupation?"

"He was a negotiator for the Culinary Workers Union of Las Vegas, they represent a wide range of job classifications including cocktail workers, bell department, kitchen workers, cooks, housekeepers, porters, and many more."

I thought of Angelo, my mob connected friend from New York who helped me in Vegas back during the Bridezilla murders. He got the union people in the casinos to help us track the killer. Maybe I would call him if necessary to see what he knows.

She continued, "He was in talks to get an increase in wages and health benefits from the owners of the casinos. There would be a big standstill in this town if they went on strike. My husband was not well liked by management in the gaming community. That's why I think he was murdered to upset the talks."

"Wouldn't they just have someone else take his position to continue the talks?"

"There's one idiot who would take over, but I believe he's in the pocket of the bosses. My husband was untouchable for kick backs and payoffs."

"Did your husband know Mr. Spenser?"

"They had been in contact for negotiations of burial benefits for the union workers and my husband was asking him for help with the arrangements for contract terms and legal information. That's why I went to him for the burial. I can't believe he's dead."

"So there was a connection between your husband and Spenser, I wonder why it would result in both their demises," I said.

"Well, I can't help you on that, my husband rarely spoke to me about his work. I just enjoyed and reaped the benefits of his occupation. I belong to a good country club and everyone in the union and its members knows me and takes care of me when I'm in any casino or hotel. Now I hope that doesn't end with his death."

I could see where her loyalty lies with her marriage. I knew she was more upset about losing her position than losing her husband. Sad state of affairs this world is in.

"Mrs. Hall do you know anyone in particular that threatened your late husband?"

"I can list you about four people who wanted him dead. I'll get a pencil and paper and write them down." She stood and went out of the room. I looked to Hannigan and said, "She took that well didn't she?"
**

Chapter 6

We left Mrs. Hall standing at her front door, yelling, "I hope you find the bastard who put me into poverty." She slammed the door as we got into my car.

Hannigan smiled and said, "I'm glad I'm not married."

"Couldn't find a good woman?"

"No, I couldn't find a good man," he said with a

grin. "Yes, I'm gay, and I don't hide it. People don't associate with a person who embalms bodies, so it doesn't matter to me if they know I'm gay also."

"I have no problem with it either, the gay thing or the embalming thing. But I do have a problem with you being Irish," I joked.

He laughed and said, "I'm only half Irish, my father, Milo Hannigan came from County Cork, Ireland but my mother was full blooded Italian, from Palermo, Italy. So I'm what I call Italish."

"I like you then. An Italish, gay embalmer, now what man wouldn't want you?"

"One who had any brains," he said with a laugh.

I dropped him back at his mortuary, and decided to go visit Deacon to see if he had anything. Then I would attack the list Mrs. Hall had given me. I arrived at Metro PD and parked, going through the back door to Lynn's office.

Deacon wasn't there, but Warren was at his desk and said to me, "Deacon was snatched by Weber and taken to his office. Poor bastard. Weber is in a mood today so most of us are trying to avoid him." He looked down the hall and saw Deacon coming towards us. "Here he comes now. I don't see any bruises."

Deacon saw me and came over, "This murder of Spenser is now a priority for me. At least until Lynn gets back. Captain knew Spenser from the burial of his brother so he wants me to find the killer fast."

"Well, I have a little info to give you about the connection between my body and your body," I said.

"We're close friends Jim, but not that close, keep

your body away from mine and we'll be just fine"
Deacon smiled.

"Funny, but you're not my type. Can we talk?"

"Well, shall we go sit while I still have a butt to
sit on?" he said with a grin. "Weber didn't chew on it
totally."

We went back to the office and sat, "I talked to
the widow of my body and she said he was a big
negotiator for the Culinary Union. He was in talks for
better pay and health benefits for the workers. The
wife thinks he was murdered because of it, and gave
me a list of suspects." I handed him the paper with
the list; he studied it.

"Well, you have a few heavy hitters here in the
management world of Vegas gambling. The wife
thinks one of these guys may have killed him?"

"That's what she believes; I'm going to talk to a
couple of them today. Now, the connection to your
body was that Hall was getting Spenser to help him
with the death benefit details for contract talks. I
wonder if they could have been plotting more than
that."

"Could be a reason to murder both. I'll have to
deputize you into helping me solve both the
murders," he said with a grin.

"You just love pushing off your work on others
don't you? I don't know why Lynn let's you hang
around."

"Because I'm so cute and cuddly. Where do you
want to start, I'll just tag along. Good things happen
when I follow you."

"You mean death and destruction? Let's hit the

list."

Deacon looked at the first name and said, "This is Morton Hackenbush, he's the big shot lawyer for the Boyd and Harrahs group of owners. These others are involved with MGM, Station and Sands groups."

"Hackenbush? Shades of Groucho Marx."

Deacon gave me a funny look, "Dr. Hugo Z. Hackenbush, played by Groucho Marx in 'A Day at the Races'," I said.

"You're just a fountain of useless information aren't you?"

I didn't respond, he was right. I just sat grinning.

We were on the road again, I let Deacon get a car out of the motor pool, we had the Dodge Charger again. It was sleek and hot and it had power that we probably wouldn't be able to use, but it was handy if we had to chase bad guys.

We went to a building off Sands Avenue and parked. The building was a nest full of lawyers, all for the gaming industry. Lots of lawsuits and contracts and buyouts around Vegas, so they needed many lawyers to sort out all the legal aspects.

We went into a lobby that looked to be gilded in gold; it screamed money and big retainers. We made our way through the potted plants and to the reception desk, where sat a gorgeous brunette in a skintight lame dress that showed her attributes quite well.

She smiled and asked if she could help us, I fantasized about what she could do for me. I stopped thinking that because Penny would interrogate me when I got home about the thoughts she could read from my mind.

"We'd like to see Hackenbush," Deacon asked flashing his badge.

She looked closely at the ID and said, "One moment." She took her phone and made a call. Shortly after, another stunning female came through a set of glass doors and up to us.

"May I help you officers?" she asked.

"It's Detective and we need to talk to Morton Hackenbush, about a homicide."

"Well, follow me please." She turned and went back through the glass doors as we followed admiring her behind. She had to know we were, she used it well.

We arrived at an office and went in to an anteroom where the girl sat back at her desk and asked us to have a seat. We went to the very plush couch and sat, as I sunk into the cushion feeling the luxury of the trappings. About ten minutes later, a man came out from behind fancy trimmed oak doors of his office.

"Gentlemen, I have a few minutes to give you if we can hurry along." He turned back and returned to his office.

I had to give an extra push to get up out of the couch, Deacon pulled me up and we went in. The office was just as luxurious as the rest of the building. I hoped this lawyer was worth every penny he put into the decorations of the room.

"Now what can I do for you gentlemen?" he said with a snug look on his face.

"I'm Detective Frank DeAngelo of LVMPD

homicide and this is Jim Richards, private investigator. We are investigating the murder of Michael Spenser, owner of Spenser Funeral Home and the possible murder of John Hall, Culinary Union rep, who I'm sure you knew," Deacon said.

"I knew of Hall, he is, or I should say was, a bulldog for union rights. We had negotiated a number of times in committee. I never dealt with him personally, sorry to have heard he is dead. Spenser was a person I only knew by reputation, he was part of the union's attempt to gain extra benefits for burial of union members."

"What was your personal opinion of either of these men," I asked.

"I have no opinions to say, I knew of these men and that is the extent of my contact with either of them. Are you questioning me in regards to their deaths? Do I need to get one of the partners in the firm to represent me?" he spoke with a smirk.

"No sir, we are just gathering information to help us find the killer. Mrs. Hall suggested we contact you since she felt you may know something of this case," I said.

"Well, Elizabeth is a fine woman, but she couldn't know much of my interest in her husband's affairs."

"Affairs? Sexual or business?" I asked.

"Please Mr. Richards; I don't feel my knowledge of Mr. or Mrs. Hall is anyone's business."

"It can be our business if you are involved in his murder," Deacon replied.

"Gentlemen, my time is precious, you need to

leave. I have no answers for you in regards to either man's death, so take it at that. Thank you and have a pleasant day." He stood and went to another door in his office and went out.

We sat there surprised by his abrupt reaction. "Touched a nerve I would say. You think he may know something more? Interesting he referred to Mrs. Hall by her first name. He evidently knows her well enough," I said to Deacon.

"Interesting that Mrs. Hall sent us to him, think she may be trying to get back at him for some reason by implicating him?" Deacon replied.

"Could be, she was not happy about losing her status in the community, so he may have something to do with his death and she's not happy about it. Don't you just love a mystery?" I said.

Deacon just gave me a stare then stood and went out of the room, I followed. He went to another door in the large building, it was marked, 'Office of Harold Kepling, Attorney at Law'. I realized it was the second name on Mrs. Hall's list.

"Well, that's convenient, we don't have to travel very far," I said.

We entered the office and did our greetings to the receptionist and she called in to Kepling. I was amazed that all these men were in their offices, did they work any court cases or just for corporations, giving them the time to sit around all day.

Kepling came out and greeted us a little warmer than Hackenbush. "Gentlemen, what can I do for Las Vegas' finest. I am a big supporter for our police; I think they take a bad rap all too often."

We went in and sat, introduced ourselves and Deacon asked, "Mr. Kepling, we're here about the death of John Hall, do you know him?"

"Hell yes, he and I golfed together twice a month, shame about his demise, really is. I have a theory as to the murderer, it was his wife."

I sat blinking in amazement, as did Deacon.
**

Chapter 7

"Why do you believe that Mrs. Hall killed her husband?" Deacon asked.

"They hated each other! He called her a gold digging bitch and she leeched off him for prestige. I tried to talk him into a divorce but he didn't have a pre-nup, idiot. Besides, she wouldn't have given him a divorce, she had too much to lose if he left her. He did have a big time life insurance policy so she'll be set for a while, plus she can sell the house for a cool mil and buy a condo on the strip. That was a marriage waiting for disaster. Too bad Johnny got the short end of the stick."

Deacon was taking all of this in; I had some things running through my mind and looked to Deacon as he asked, "How would she have killed him? Coroner says he died of natural causes."

"She was a natural cause for his death. She kept him drunk hoping he would have an accident in his car. I don't know how she reached out while he was at the union negotiations, I saw him take the dive into the guacamole, messy stuff. Poor bastard. I gave my statement to the police, but they didn't investigate when it came up that he died of natural causes."

"Was her whole life revolving around her social contacts?" I asked.

"Of course, John said it himself many times. You want to know what I think? I have the feeling she was whoring around. I can't prove it, she knows I was friends with John, so I wasn't in on her playmates. Check that out, she may have hired someone to kill him with some fast acting poison that hides in the body, undetectable to an autopsy."

I thought that this guy had a great imagination, which makes him a good lawyer. If you don't have the facts, make it up. Deacon was now taking notes in his little black book, I probably should carry one, with my memory, but I keep forgetting to buy one. I'll have to remember the untraceable poison idea and talk to Joe Lang.

"Mr. Kepling, what happens to the union and management talks now that Hall is out of the picture?" I asked.

He sat for a moment and then said, "Todd Cramer will take his spot, he's the second in line to handle negotiations and I think he'll drag out the talks. I've never liked him, most of us don't. Not because we are the enemy on the other side of the war lines, he just has too many irons in the fire. He is on the take from what I hear, nothing to be proven, but the word is there. I don't trust the man and neither should you."

"Why would anyone want the talks to drag on?" Deacon asked.

"Well, the word is that Culinary may go on strike if the talks stall. Do you know what that would do to this city? Just about every hotel and casino will have to be serviced by management. Can you see some upper management boss cleaning rooms? Not to mention that food service would take hours to get people fed. John Hall played hard ball and he threatened a strike; Cramer will kiss ass and keep the talks going forever to please the casino owners."

"So someone wanted Hall dead because he could kill business around town due to a strike." I said.

"Bingo. As a representative for management and the owners, I can't say what my personal feelings are about this, I'd like to see this drag out myself. But we aren't too close to finalizing anything."

"A motive for murder would be to get Hall out of the way to prevent the city from shutting down. Do you think anyone in your camp would stoop to murder?" I asked.

He laughed, "I think half of these corporate owners would have been glad to murder him, but no, I can't say I could pin this on any of my clients."

"What about lawyers?" Deacon asked with a smile.

"I can give you names of every lawyer in these talks who would have loved to murder Hall, but I don't think they did it either. I have no idea why he was murdered, if he didn't die of natural causes."

"Spenser was just a funeral director and he was only involved in helping Hall set up the details for burial benefits, have any idea on his death?" Deacon asked.

"I only saw Spenser once when he came into the talks to explain the burial benefit details to management. He was there for a couple hours and then left. I can't put any speculation on his death."

Deacon handed him his card and said, "Thanks for your candor, please call if you think of anything that may help us find the murderer."

"My pleasure gentlemen, if you ever need a lawyer, I'm open to all aspects of law defense. Thanks for listening to me prattle. I hope you find the killer, John was a good friend."

We stood and Deacon and I went out. I looked at the next two names on the list and asked Deacon, "Think we'll find anything from the other names?"

"Since we're here, may as well talk." He turned and went to a door down the hall, the next name on the list.

We got nothing out of the them, they clammed up when we started talking murder. The last man was actually rude, but we didn't think he had anything to tell anyway. We left the building and sat in the car.

"So we have a lot of information that really tells us not much. Okay, he could have been snuffed for the sake of saving the city from loss of revenue for the corporations and their stockholders. Is preventing a strike really enough for murder?" Deacon said.

"The joys of detecting. Seeking out the clues and piecing them together, to find a killer. Now don't you wish Lynn were here?" I said with a grin.

"Yes, mostly to get Webber off my butt. Lynn

has a better butt to chew," he said.

I looked at him and grinned, "You would know about chewing her butt."

"Let's not go there. Now where shall we check out next?"

"You're the official detective, you tell me. I'm thinking we go talk to Hall's replacement, Todd Cramer. Maybe we can rattle his tree to see what falls out."

"Sounds like a plan," Deacon said and put the car in gear, drove out and then said, "Just where do we find him before I put on more mileage?"

I pulled my cell phone and called Lacey. She came on and I asked her to look in the city phone book for Todd Cramer. I heard her moving around and then could hear paper rustling. She was quiet for a moment then gave me a number and said the address was not listed. I thanked her and hung up. Deacon had pulled into a Carl's Jr restaurant and parked.

He wrote down the number in his book and said, "It's almost dinner time, let's grab a bite to eat and finish in the morning. I'm tired out."

"You're always tired out, but food sounds good, I didn't have much for lunch with Penny at Bistro's today." We exited the car and went in to grab some burgers and fries. We sat at a table by the window so Deacon could watch the car. I didn't think anyone would steal a cop car, but it was a hot Dodge charger. We wolfed down our food and sat back relaxing.

"So, Hall was negotiating contract talks with management. He threatened to strike and shut down the city. Management definitely didn't want this, so one of them, or more, would have wanted him out of the picture, enough to murder him. I can see that, but why Spenser?" Deacon was mumbling as he sat back in the hard wooden chairs.

"I'm wondering if Spenser had anything to do with Hall's murder. Maybe it's just a coincidence that some disgruntled customer killed him around the time Hall took a dive into the guacamole," I replied.

Could be, it's just a hook that they both had dealings with each other. But you're right it may be a coincidence. Either way, I'm going back to the precinct to sign out for the day, avoid Weber and go back to my lonely little apartment, thinking about Lynn sitting in her luxury hotel in LA. Life is unjust at times."

"Well, you won't go for a hooker so you'll just have to take matters into your own hand."

"You're disgusting. I'm outta here." He stood as I was laughing and we went out to the car. Deacon dropped me off to my car and I said I'd see him in the morning and got into my car. I carefully turned it on hoping it wouldn't blow up, sending me to my funeral like in my dream. I still got chills thinking about being in the closed coffin, I wasn't good at confined spaces, so I definitely wasn't happy about it.

I drove back to my humble home and thought about Mrs. Hall, and what Kepling said about her screwing around. He also said that she probably wouldn't murder him to keep her social standing, but the insurance money and the property was a good motive. I'd have to check on her a little more.

I pulled into the garage and parked, going into the house finding Willy gulping down his kibble. Penny came bouncing out from somewhere when she heard me, latching on to me with a big wet kiss.

"Guess who I have on my show tomorrow?"

"I have no idea, who?"

"I have the Las Vegas Funeral Directors Co-operative Association. To discuss the cost of funerals and options for burial. Would you like to come in to model a coffin or two?"

I just stood there in wonderment at my wife's sense of humor.

**

Chapter 8

"You are one sick puppy," I said as I pushed her back carefully, "I'm not even going to go there when it comes to coffins. I've had a day of enough death and lawyers, two of the same thing, by the way. I want to crash on the couch, open a couple beers and fool around with my wife. Have you seen her? Good-looking woman, natural golden brown hair, well built for sex. She's not one who messes with her husband's head. If you see her send her to the couch," I said and went to the living room and plopped on the couch. Willy jumped up and plopped down on my lap.

Penny was humming as she nuked a couple beef meat pasties in the microwave, my favorite, especially smothered with ketchup. She was good with a microwave, cooking was a task for her, but she could throw a good microwave dinner together in just under twenty minutes.

She set up a couple folding tables and put a plate with my food in front of me and an open can of beer. I loved this woman.

She sat with her food and we watched television, a good comedy that I really needed, "Evan Almighty". It was a goofy movie, but I was misty-eyed happy as it progressed. I didn't like "The Office" with Steve Carell, but he was funny in this movie. Around eleven we went to bed, Willy jumped up on his Bate's motel chair that I bought for him from the magic convention murder case. He circled and then flopped down with a huff.

Penny crawled under the covers and cuddled me. We lay there in each other's arms and she whispered to me, "I am happy every day to be with you. I would never put you in a coffin; I know you don't want that. I wouldn't want that either. Please don't dream about death tonight, I want you alive in the morning to kiss me before I go to work."

I smiled and kissed her forehead as we both fell asleep.

~~*~~

It was late when Trapper and Sam returned to the Denver Hills Bed and Breakfast and entered the small lobby finding Mrs. Walters asleep in her rocking chair behind the counter. Trapper and Sam stood at the desk as he softly cleared his throat, bringing Mrs.

Walters out of her sleep. She brought her grey-haired head up from her slumber, looked surprised and stood as slowly as her eighty-some year old body would let her.

"My goodness, I don't usually fall asleep at the desk, but I was concerned about the young couple who fought earlier, so I waited here to see if he would come back, but the young man didn't come back, or I didn't see him. It's been quiet this evening. Did you two have a good meal?"

Sam answered, "It was fantastic, and your recommendation was spot on. Afterwards we went to a very nice bar down the road from the restaurant and listened to some good jazz music. It was a very enjoyable evening for our first night in Denver. Thank you."

"Well, I'm glad you kids enjoyed yourselves. We serve a continental breakfast in the dining room at exactly eight-thirty in the morning, so don't be late."

Trapper said they would be there, then they left Mrs. Walters as he and Sam went up the stairs to their room. As they reached the floor, they headed down the hall towards the end, where their room was, Trapper noticed a slightly open door. He stopped and pushed the door with his finger and saw something that he didn't want to see. A bloody dead body stretched out on the bed, it was the young woman.

He carefully pushed Sam back so she didn't see the body and told her to go down and call the police, quickly. She stared at him, then realized he was being serious and quickly ran back downstairs to call the police, trusting Trapper's request. He yelled to her before she was all the way down to say there was a murder. She felt a chill when she heard that.

About an hour later the Denver police, their medical examiner and the forensic people were on the scene. Trapper, Sam and Mrs. Walters were in a sitting room off the lobby talking to a Detective Scott Peters of the Denver Police.

"So, getting this straight, you went to dinner after the couple came down the stairs arguing, so you didn't see what transpired after the blowout?"

Trapper answered, "They fought, I tried to intervene but they stormed off, she went back upstairs, he went out the door. We arrived back later and I found the body through the open door of their room."

"You were a homicide cop up in Michigan, correct?" Peters asked Trapper.

"Yep, homicide Detective Lieutenant, retired; now I'm working private out in Vegas. With a firm there run by a friend," he replied.

"I've always wanted to go to Vegas, never found the time. Is it as good as they say?" he asked.

"Better," Trapper said with a smile. "I grew up there, until I moved to Michigan. You should try it sometime."

"I will, now back to the murder; you didn't know the couple before tonight? The male is identified as Terrence Rice and the woman is, or was Linda Foster."

"No, we just came across them in the lobby when they fought. We left shortly after, as I said, and didn't see either one after that. At least until we came back and I found the woman dead in the room."

"Why did you look in the room?"

"Well, being an ex-cop I was curious about an open door, I carefully pushed the door open and saw her on the bed, blood all around her. I asked my girlfriend to call the police, she did."

"Well, I have all I need. Mrs. Walters, my mom is a friend of yours, so I don't figure you would murder anyone," he said with a smile.

"Scotty, you tell your mother that I said hello and you can never tell if I could murder anyone," she said with a sly smile.

Trapper liked this woman. Detective Peters stood and said, "Okay, I'll wait and see what CSU comes up with, but I would recommend that you stay alert in case Rice comes back again. Although I don't think he will."

Peters was heading out of the sitting room followed by Trapper, Sam and Mrs. Walters just as the front door opened and in came Terrence Rice. Trapper moved Sam and Mrs. Walters back with his arm and called to Peters that he was the man. Peters pulled his service revolver and told Rice to drop to the floor. The young man looked shocked and dropped to his knees after seeing a gun pointed at him. He had his hands up in the air as Peters pulled them back and cuffed him. Peters called for his uniforms and told them to watch him until he said to take him in.

Peters knelt down to Rice and asked, "Where have you been tonight?"

The shocked looking young man said, "I was at a

55

bar, getting drunk."

"Any witnesses?"

"Yeah, some hooker I picked up, I spent the last couple hours with her."

"I don't suppose you can give me the name of this hooker?"

"Yes sir, her name was Brandy."

Sam smiled and whispered to Trapper, "Odds are that it's a fake name."

~~*~~

The next morning I awoke feeling strange, I thought about Trapper for some reason. I would have to call him to see how his trip was going.

I kissed my wife as she stretched to wake. She kissed me back and said good morning. We both got out of bed and went to our own bathrooms to get ready. That was the nice thing about having our own bathrooms; we can get ready for the day without having to stumble over each other. Although I liked to join her in her shower when the mood was right, this morning it wasn't. I was shaved and ready for the world, as I went out to get my morning toast I could smell something delicious. I entered the kitchen and found Penny making French toast. I was amazed.

She smiled and put a plate of French toast in front of me as I sat at the snack bar. "Boney appetite, my love," she said with a smirk now.

I liked French toast so I dug in. It was good.

"So are you going after your killers today?" she asked.

"I'm going to see Deacon, then we will go chase after killers, or so I hope."

"Well, be careful. I'm not ready to be a widow," she laughed

I got my things ready after Penny left to go to her show. I had custody of Willy, so that meant I had to go to the office to drop him off for Lacey to watch him. I took him to my car and started it up with trepidation, wondering when it would blow up, if at all. Willy sat next to me as I drove to the office and parked. I let Willy follow me into the building; he was being carried too much and needed the exercise.

I went by Trapper's office but I knew he would be out, then to Buck's office, but he wasn't in either. I went to the lobby and before I realized I forgot to announce my arrival and totally scared Lacey when I popped out of the hallway and said, "Hi."

"Damn it! Do you have to do that to me! It was so deathly quiet in here, and then you jump out on me!"

"I didn't jump!" I defended myself. "I just came out of the back."

"Yes, do you realize that hallway opening is so dark, it is spooky? I don't like spooky!" she lamented.

"Okay, I'll have a light and an alarm installed to let you know when someone is approaching."

"Fine! Now Deacon called and asked you to meet him at the Hannigan Mortuary, he said he called your cell phone but it went to voice mail."

I must have been in the shower when he called. I thanked her, ruffled Willy's head and went back to my car.

Chapter 9

As I drove out, I checked my cell phone for the voice mail and found my phone was shut off. Strange, I don't remember shutting it off, but the joy of forgetfulness was plaguing me more every day. I just hope I never got Alzheimers. I don't think I would like to forget who Penny was or Deacon and Lynn. I felt for the families of people who had the disease, it must be tough.

I turned the phone on, found Deacon's voice mail, and listened to it. He explained that since he was now putting Hall's disappearance together with Spenser's murder, he got CSI to go to the mortuary and check it out. I pulled into the parking lot and went into the building finding the same pleasant woman at the reception desk. She waved and said to go in, the police were still there.

I went in the door I had gone through a number of times in the last couple days and I went back to the cold room, as I called it, and found Deacon talking to Larry, the supervisor of the CSI techs. There were a couple of forensic people working on the drawer that Hall had been in. Deacon saw me, smiled and waved me over.

"Good morning, I tried to wake you but got your voice mail, not answering your phone in the mornings now?"

"No, it was turned off for some reason, I didn't do it, at least I think I didn't."

"Not a good sign, Jim, memory loss. You need to

carry a note pad and write everything down."

"Like you do, are you suffering from memory loss?"

"I have many facts to process, so I need to write things down."

"Okay, whatever you say, now what have you found so far?"

Larry said, "We have pulled a good number of prints from the drawers and luckily the bag that the body was brought in was still here. Hannigan did some checking and found that he is missing a couple body wraps so we know what to look for. The door was jimmied at the back and the thief left a couple good prints on the door, we just need to compare them to our database. I'll give you a call when we have something," he said to Deacon and went off to do his work.

"So you are taking over my case now?" I asked.

"No, just gathering facts for you to investigate, but I'll tag along and help. You may turn up something to help me catch my murderer."

"Sounds good. Now I'm a substitute for Lynn, she leads, you follow. But you can't have sex with me."

Deacon leaned in and started making smooching noises; I pushed him away. "Don't be that way honey," he said.

"Screw you, no I'm not."

Hannigan walked in and saw me, coming over he said, "Mr. Richards, thank you for getting the police to help with this."

"Well, much of the credit goes to my friend

Detective DeAngelo."

"Now you'll have to excuse me I still have bodies to process. The work never ends."

"As long as they keep dying, you'll be busy," I said.

"Yes, there's an endless supply. Thanks and if you need me I'll be up to my elbows in body parts." He left the room and Deacon turned to me and said, "Shall we go back to Metro?"

I followed him out and into the precinct parking. We were walking towards the building when Warren came out the back entrance door.

"Hey Greg, What's up?" Deacon asked.

"It's good in there; Weber is at another meeting about the President coming to Vegas next week. The place is full of Secret Service all explaining and checking out our operation. We've done well enough in the past protecting dignitaries coming into town. Hell, Paris Hilton feels safe here, doesn't she?" He laughed out loud and went off.

"Why is the President coming here?" I asked.

"He's stumping for Senator Rose, trying to get him re-elected. And showing Vegas that he cares about our economic crunch."

"Most of these casino owners could keep this country going for years with their cash flow. Maybe the President needs a loan from the Maloofs."

Deacon shook his head and walked away from me, "Or he wants to gamble using the national debt as collateral, he may be able to play one hand of twenty-one," I yelled to him and followed.

We went into Lynn's office, "Any word from

Lynn about her return?" I asked.

"Trial is going into overtime; she's a key witness and has to stay till the end. I'm holding up better, I'm getting used to her being away."

Deacon picked up his phone and dialed a number, waited, then asked for Larry. "Hey Larry, its Deacon, any hits on the prints?"

He listened and then hung up, turned to the fax machine in the office and waited. After a few minutes, two sheets of paper came out and Deacon pulled both. He read the papers and handed them to me.

"There were two distinctive prints and two people using that door. I was told by Hannigan that no one used that door, so any fresh prints would have to be the thieves and possibly murderers."

I saw the pictures, neither of them looked like thugs, and neither looked familiar, but why would they? One was named Harry Brinkley and the other was Mercer Thaning. "Are we going to go after them now?"

"We have the addresses on the papers, I'll call for a couple warrants to search for bodies and we'll go." He made a couple calls and we waited. About an hour later, Warren came in and gave Deacon some papers, "These were just delivered, shall I get a team together to make an assault?"

"Sounds good, have them meet in the back parking in a few minutes." He turned to me and said, "Let's go bust some grave robbers."

"Technically, they didn't rob a grave yet," I offered.

"Do you always have to be so literal? Let's go."

We went out to the back as a few cops were gathering and Deacon went over the plan. Everyone headed to their cars and the stragglers caught up. I went with Deacon and we drove out to Valley View and into a neighborhood that didn't look poor. I thought that crime was paying well, at least for criminals.

Everyone congregated in front of the first house on the warrants and then Deacon went to the door, pounding on it and yelling to open up. No answer. Deacon tried the door, it was locked so he signaled the uniform with the ram and he took out the door in one hit. Everyone flowed into the building and started to clear the place. They found no one in the residence and then Deacon called in the rest of the uniforms to search the house for a body. I wasn't sure if they would stash the body here, or just dump it out in the desert. But then I didn't know what the intent of taking the body was for.

"It's clear and we found no body," one of the uniforms reported to Deacon after about a half hour of searching.

Deacon said, "Okay, three uniforms stay here to see if the perp returns, if he does, bring him in. Let's go to the second location."

We arrived at the second house and Deacon did his door pounding, then the door opened and a woman of about twenty, looked shocked to see so many police.

"Is Mercer Thaning here?" Deacon asked.

The woman was visibly shaken and said, he was

out. Deacon handed her the warrant and told one of the uniforms to watch her as everyone went into the building. The woman was stammering about this being illegal and the cop watching her told her to read the search warrant, she did and shut up.

About ten minutes later, one cop yelled from the basement and we all went down. He pointed to a huge freezer in one corner and opened it to show the body all stuffed in it, frozen like a side of beef. Deacon read the toe tag, it had Hall's name and it read "Hannigan Mortuary" on the bottom of it.

"Looks like we found Hall, now we need to find Thaning," Deacon said. "Get the coroner down here to take the body out." Deacon turned to me, "You can call Hannigan to let him know the body was found."

I went off to the side of the basement and called him, he came on after a couple rings and I told him the body has been recovered. He was ecstatic and asked when he could get it back. "Well, it's been frozen, and kind of all in a fetal position, they've called the coroner down to take the body out, so call Joe Lang for the disposition of the corpse." He thanked me and we finished the call. I went back to Deacon.

"I put a BOLO out for Thaning, we need to talk to the woman." We went upstairs and the cop watching the woman had her in the living room. She looked scared as Deacon sat next to her on the couch.

"What's your name?"

"Lana," she replied.

"Are you related to Mercer Thaning?"

"I'm his housekeeper. I was here to clean today, that's all I know."

"Do you know where Mr. Thaning is at the moment?"

"I assume he is at work."

"Where does he work?"

"Wittly, Danner, Thaning and Benson, Attorneys at Law. Up on Sands Avenue."

Deacon turned to me, smiled and said, "The same building we were at yesterday. Kepling was so close when he said there were murderous lawyers."

**

Chapter 10

Denver police held Terrence Rice over night as they ran his background check and held him on suspicion of murder. Detective Peters called and asked Trapper if he'd like to sit in on the questioning. Trapper said he appreciated the thought and accepted, so he drove to the precinct after he dropped Sam at the clinic to go visit her brother. He told her he would be back later and to call if there was a problem.

Trapper arrived at Denver PD, went to the front desk and asked for Detective Peters. The officer on the desk called back and Peters came up to get Trapper.

"Thanks for coming, I'd like to get your take on this since you were on the scene before and after it happened."

Rice was sitting in the interrogation room looking frazzled; he must have had a bad night's sleep. Trapper would have thought they could have questioned Rice last night, but he figured they do things the way they want here in Denver. He was not a cop in Michigan anymore.

Peters sat across from Rice as Trapper stood back watching. Rice would look to Trapper every few seconds, as if he remembered him from his altercation with the girl.

"Terrence, tell me what happened last night?" Peters asked and went silent.

He sat looking frightened, staring around the room, not focusing on anything in particular. He still glanced at Trapper occasionally and then would quickly look away. Trapper had seen enough of this to know he was hiding something, nervous movements and avoidance.

"Come on Terrence, talk, what happened to Linda Foster?" Peters demanded.

"I don't know, really I don't. I didn't even know she was dead until the cop gave me my rights, he said I was being arrested on suspicion of murder. I didn't do it, honestly, I loved Linda."

Trapper, cleared his throat and said, "Then why did you spit at her and call her a psycho bitch?"

The man jumped slightly when Trapper spoke, he looked away from both of the men, "I was pissed at her, she was getting on me about her going alone to a meeting she had with a potential job interview. She had this thing about always yelling at me for every little thing, I just snapped at that moment, but I still loved her, and I didn't kill her."

"What Job interview, and why so late at night?"

"It was more of a business dinner, to meet her potential employer. They set it up and she wanted to go alone, I didn't like that she was meeting some guy in a bar for food and drinks, I wanted to go, she told me to stay. We argued about it. That's all. After this guy separated us in the lobby," he said looking to Trapper, then back to Peters, "I went out and got drunk. I picked up some hooker and we talked the night, I didn't even do anything with her, that's how much I loved Linda. I came back to get arrested by you."

"What bar did you go to Terrence?"

"I don't know, it was within walking distance, small, dark, had a lot of women hanging around, probably hookers. I think the sign said, 'The Happy Hour', I think."

Peters smiled and sat back, "That bar should be called the Gay Hour, because it's a lesbian bar. You were in the company of lesbians, dykes and trannies."

That drew Trapper's attention. He was waist deep in gender issues and now a lesbian bar surfaces.

Terrence looked shocked and said, "You telling me I sat with some chick with a dick?"

"Possible, if she showed interest in you then I'd say she was one, yes."

"Oh man, I opened up my heart to her, he, whatever...."

"You said her name was Brandy, we'll check it out and get back to you." Peters waved to the uniformed cop watching from outside and he came in to take Terrence back to a cell.

"Feel like taking a ride?" Peters asked Trapper.

"Sure, I have some confession time too." They went out of the precinct and to a car at the back of the building. Peters got behind the wheel as Trapper buckled in. Trapper explained his reason for being in Denver, making Peters smile even more.

"You just are having a gender adventure aren't you?"

Trapper laughed, "Yep, I've been in enough gay bars in the last month to make up for all my adventures in my youth. I had a few gay friends on the force, like what they should say in the military, 'Don't ask, don't care', and I didn't care, they were good cops."

"Was this in Michigan or Las Vegas?" Peters asked.

"Both, Vegas and Michigan. You seem to know a lot about me, did you check me out?"

"Yep, I wanted to see if you were clean, you were, by the way. I pulled your sheet and you've had a distinguished past."

"And proud of every minute of it," Trapper said with a grin, "What's the gender scene around here?"

"There's a community of gay and transgendered near here, it's safe and we take care of their rights. I'm kind of on the side of trannies, they hold a fascination for me," he said with a sideways glance to Trapper.

"Well, I'll have to introduce you to my girlfriend's brother, uh, soon to be sister."

They both laughed as they pulled into the

parking lot of the Happy Hour, parked and went in.

The bull dyke at the door smiled and said, "Hey Scotty, long time, how you doing?"

"I'm doing fine," Peters smiled to Trapper, then back to the burly woman, "Chris, need some info, I'm on a case of murder."

"Sure, anything for you, what's up?" She spoke with a distinct man's voice. Trapper would have thought she was a man if it hadn't been for the deep cleavage in the tank top.

"Is there a girl here who hangs out, goes by Brandy?"

"We got two. Take your pick."

"One who was here last night letting some slub cry on her shoulder about his broken heart?"

"Ah, yes, the weeper. He was with Brandy Delight, one of our drag queens from the show. We had no show last night, so Brandy was relaxing. I remember him, scrawny guy with dirty brown hair and pointy nose."

"Yep, sounds like our man. Thanks, Chris." He started to turn, Chris asked, "Aren't you coming in for a quick drink Scotty, for old time sake? You don't come around as much as you used to."

Peters cleared his throat, "I'm on duty, can't indulge."

Trapper grabbed his arm and pulled him into the room, saying, "Well, I'm not on duty, you can drink soda pop, let's check this out." They entered the room as Trapper was laughing at Peters' embarrassment.

As they sat at the bar, numerous women walked by all greeting Peters. He got a smile on his face,

"Okay, I come here a lot, or used to. I was nearly seen by one of the patrol cops who came in to check out a complaint of theft. He was in the door before I saw him, I don't think he saw me, but I was careful after that."

"Not that they'd make a big deal out of you being in a lesbian bar. Lots of men hold a fascination for them."

"Yeah, well the cops in my precinct are all mountain men types, the old boy's club. Denver, Rocky Mountain high, and all that. I'm one of the younger crowd, the new blood in the force and more tolerant of alternate lifestyles."

"We were about the same out in Michigan. There weren't many gay clubs but the ones that were there were all safe."

"Well, our boy's alibi checks out, now I have to find out who wanted to kill the girl. Couldn't be a robbery, Mrs. Walters was asleep at the door, she didn't come to harm, so it had to be personal against the girl," Peters said as he drank from his cola.

Trapper hoisted his beer and said, "They weren't from around here were they?"

"Nope, their driver's licenses said they came in from Oakley, Kansas, a straight shot out route 70. I guess Dorothy isn't in Kansas anymore."

"You're quoting the Wizard of Oz and hanging in gay bars, should I be concerned?"

"Hey, I'm all male and I can prove it," Peters said.

"Just keep it in your pants, I believe you. Shall we go back and break Terrence out of jail?"

"I'm already out of here," Peters said and stood. Trapper downed the rest of his beer and they went to the exit, saying good-bye to Chris.

They arrived back at the precinct and parked out back. Once in the building they found some commotion going on and Peters asked a uniform what was happening.

"Some prisoner got his hands on the holding cell guard's weapon and is holding off everyone."

"Crap, Terrence just couldn't wait till we got back," Peters was heading to the holding cells followed by Trapper. They got to the barred door and Peters told the guard to open up. They went in and Peters came up to the entrance of the cells by two other cops holding weapons.

Peters yelled into the hallway, "Terrence, I'm Detective Peters, I talked to you earlier. I just got back and we established your alibi. We know that you didn't kill your girlfriend. Now put down the weapon and come out. This can go wrong if you don't."

They heard nothing, and then a voice said quietly, "I'm coming out."
   **

Chapter 11

Deacon and I were back at the law offices on Sands Avenue, and went in with a few extra uniformed officers to back us up. They spread out in the lobby as Deacon went to the reception desk asking for the directions to Thaning's office. He had a warrant for Thaning's arrest for theft and illegal storage of human remains along with suspicion of murder.

The receptionist looked nervous and said she would call Mr. Thaning to let him know they were here.

"I wouldn't do that unless you want to be arrested for aiding a felon. Just point us to his office and keep your hands off the phone," Deacon said with a growl.

She gave him directions and he thanked her. We went through the glass doors and down the hall to Thaning's office where we were met by another secretary.

"Is Thaning in?" Deacon asked. The girl said he was and Deacon led his officers to the door and in. Thaning was shocked to see the police as he sat with a man also looking shocked.

"Mercer Thaning, you are under arrest for breaking and entering, theft, possession and illegally storing a corpse and suspicion of murder. Please stand," Deacon spoke as he went around the desk to Thaning. The lawyer stood and Deacon placed the cuffs on him, handing him over to one of the uniforms to be taken out.

The man sitting with Thaning called to him, "I'll get Wittly to represent you. We'll have you out in no time." Deacon gave him a nasty glare and the man gave a defiant look back to him.

Deacon muttered, "I hate lawyers," as we departed the office.

Mortuary Murders

Terrence Rice came out of the holding cell with his hands in the air. He left the gun in the cell and Peters told the guard to go retrieve it. Rice was pounced upon by two other cops and was roughly handled.

"Hey, ease off on him, now!" Peters ordered, the cops looked to him as one said, "He grabbed a gun and held us off."

"Did he fire the gun?"

"No, he just waved it around," was his answer.

"And why did he even get hold of your gun?" he spoke to the guard holding his retrieved weapon.

"Well, I … uh… I guess I wasn't watching closely."

"Ok, just so I don't have to report your carelessness, let's just mark this off as a controlled incidence and get back to your duties. I'll take Mr. Rice and since we have established that he committed no crime other than being stupid, I'm processing him out. Is that all right with you?" he spoke again to the guard who lost his weapon.

"Sure, Lieutenant, that's just fine with us." He looked to the other cops as they let Rice go.

Peters grabbed Terrence Rice's arm and pulled him out of the holding area. He took Rice and Trapper back to his office and sat Rice down in a chair.

"Listen carefully, Terrence, we established your alibi, you were with a drag queen last night when your girlfriend was murdered. Now we have to find out why. Did she have any enemies or some person who'd want to murder her?"

Rice sat looking disturbed then said, "No, everyone loved Linda, she was the salt of the earth and kind. I don't know anybody who'd even want to hurt her."

"Tell me again about you're reason for being in Denver."

"Linda had a job interview with some guy from Denver Telecom to talk about a customer service management position here. If she got the job, we would have gotten married and moved here. That was our plan." He started to tear up and then broke down. Peters handed him a tissue from a box on his desk and waited for him to come around.

"You said that you argued about her going to see this guy alone, do you know if she met with him?"

"No, I came back when you arrested me, I don't know if she even left the bed and breakfast."

"Give me the name of the man she was supposed to meet and then you can go."

"I heard her say his name was Harvey Gentry, he was some supervisor at Denver Telecom."

"What is Denver Telecom?"

"They're an outsource call center for T-Mobile, they take customer service calls about phone service and billing. Linda did that in our city, but the pay wasn't that good. She was offered a management position and increase in pay here."

"Ok, write down a cell phone number I can reach you at. You do have a cell phone?"

"Sure, Linda got it for me from her last job." He

wrote down the number on the pad Peters handed him.

"Okay, stay available, don't leave town without arranging to have the body taken back home. I probably want to talk to you some more."

Rice stood and Peters called a uniform to process him out and give him a ride back to the B&B.

Trapper spoke, "Now the real detecting begins."

~~*~~

Thaning sat in interrogation room three as Deacon and I watched him through the trick glass. He was fidgeting and looking nervous.

"He should be used to interrogation rooms if he's been here to talk with clients," I said.

"Nope, he's a corporate flunky, he handles business dealings. The closest he probably got to criminals is the other lawyers in his building."

"Now what would a lawyer want with a dead body? Too early for Halloween." I joked.

"Well, I'm going to find out. Wait here so Mr. Lawyer doesn't complain about a civilian being in on the questioning."

I said I would wait and Deacon went out of observation. He entered the room and sat across from Thaning, who was trying to keep his composure.

"Mr. Thanking, you are being charged with breaking and entering a mortuary, theft of a corpse, hiding the corpse in your basement and suspicion of murder of a funeral director. You've been busy."

"I'm not speaking until my lawyer gets here."

"You are a lawyer, you aren't going to represent yourself?"

"I don't handle criminal law, Wittly does."

"So you are saying that you have committed a crime?"

"Nothing of the sort, you have little to go on."

"We have your prints on the door to the mortuary, and we found the stolen body in your meat freezer in your basement. I'd say we have enough to go on, wouldn't you?"

He went silent, just giving Deacon a hard cold stare. "You have just committed minor felonies, but I'm interested in the murder of Michael Spenser, the funeral director who turned over your stolen body to the mortuary for embalming. Coincidence that the two are connected. You know anything about Spenser's death?"

"I have already said that I'm not saying anything till my lawyer gets here."

"Play it your way, we have you on the B&E, theft and illegal storage of a corpse. So plan to spend some time in jail, I hope your corporate interests will understand." Deacon sat waiting, Thaning made no attempt to speak so Deacon stood and walked out of the room.

Deacon came back into observation and said again, "I hate lawyers."

We sat on the chairs in the room watching Thaning through the glass. "Hall was a person who Thaning would have known through negotiations with the union, why would he want his body? Maybe to keep something from being found? But Joe Lang autopsied the body and found nothing out of the ordinary. It may be a good idea to have him double check the body after he thaws."

"I already asked Joe to do that when we met at Thaning's home. Joe said he'd give him a good going over this time. He admitted that the signs pointed to natural causes so he didn't give the body a really close look."

"Joe's a good ME, but he's overworked. Have you seen the morgue? It's piled up with bodies. I can see that he'd be in a hurry to push them through."

"Well, he'll do it right this time."

A uniform came to the door and told us that Thaning's lawyer was in, Deacon said to put him in with Thaning. He went out and a minute later, a man we presumed was Wittly entered the room. Deacon still had the cameras and sound on in the room as we watched the two men.

"What the hell did you do, Mercer? I read the charges and this is serious." He stopped, looked to the cameras and saw the red light was on; he went to tap on the glass and said, "If you are in there watching, stop it. I need time to talk to my client." He just stood glaring at the glass as Deacon reached over and shut the cameras down. Wittly looked up to the camera, satisfied it was off, then pulled the venetian blinds in the room and we saw no more of them.

We just sat talking, waiting for something to happen.

"Any word from Lynn?" I asked.

"Yep, she's still out in LA waiting to be called to testify, if at all. I hope she gets back soon."

"Well, hang in there, you can do it," I said just as the venetian blinds were pulled up and Wittly tapped on the glass, yelling for Deacon to come back in. He grinned to me, turned the camera back on and stood, going out of the room and into interrogation.

He sat as the two men stared with stoney faces. "So, what's up?" Deacon asked Wittly.

"My client wants to cut a deal. His testimony on Spenser's murder for dropping the charges on B&E and possession of the body."

"Well, now you'll have to wait until I can get the DA in here." Deacon stood and went out.

   **

Chapter 12

About a half hour later, the Assistant District Attorney, Webb Morse, came in and Deacon explained the whole incident to him. He grinned widely and said, "Damn, I love seeing Thaning squirm, I never liked the guy. Can we wait another half hour to make him suffer?"

Deacon laughed, "You have all the cards, deal when you're ready. Jim, would you like to join me for some refreshments?"

I said I would and we went to the break room where I punched the button for a hot chocolate on one of the two machines, and Deacon got coffee on the other. We waited for the slow moving machines to dispense the drinks as Deacon said, "I'm getting a feeling that Thaning will be able to tell us what we need to know, he seems to be such a weasel, I'm betting he will give us what we need."

"I hope so for your sake, we don't have much to go on, but my case has been solved, I got the body to be returned to my client."

"I'm happy for you, now you can solve my case."

"Again you want me to do your job for you. I'm telling Lynn." He gave me a finger hidden by his body and we got our drinks, took them back to the observation room and found the ADA sitting on a chair grinning at the glass.

"Okay I think we've made them sweat enough, they both look ready to pluck." He stood and went out, then into the interrogation room followed by Deacon. Wittly stood as he saw Morse enter. "Well, Webb, how fortunate that they sent you."

"Dan, I wouldn't get too excited yet, until I hear your proposal," Morse replied.

"Simple, my client will give you the necessary information about the murder of Michael Spenser in return for dropping the charges he is facing." Wittly gave Morse a big toothy smile, his shark's teeth all white and sharp.

"I'll cut him a deal only if his info is good and pans out, otherwise he can sit in a cell until next year."

Wittly turned to Thaning and gave him a wink, "Sounds good to me, how about you?"

Thaning said, "Fine, whatever, just get me out of here."

Deacon told everyone to sit and said to Thaning,

"You have been read your rights and your statements are being recorded, so Webb, start the dealings."

Webb Morse spoke, "All right, you have knowledge of the murder of Michael Spenser and I'm willing to make a deal for the information to drop charges pending against you. Now this knowledge doesn't include you directly involved in the murder of Spenser, does it?"

"No, I was not directly involved; I just had knowledge of the crime," Thaning replied.

"All right, this conversation is being recorded for the record and you swear that you are giving truthful statements?"

"I will."

"Fine, so talk."

Thaning looked a bit nervous now, probably from thinking about the repercussions of ratting out the criminals who committed the murder. He looked to Deacon, "What I tell you won't go out of this room? You can use the info to find the killers, but I don't want my name dragged out from it. These people are fanatical and dangerous."

"I'll do my best to keep you out of it," Deacon said.

Thaning sat for a moment then said, "Harry Brinkley and I were deep into debt to certain people who backed our gambling habits."

"Bookies?" Morse asked.

"They were more than the small independent books, they were a little more mob related, I think. Harry found then through one of his contacts in the system."

"System? The criminal system? He had contacts with criminals who were married to the mob?"

"Yeah, that's what Harry said. He got us backing and we lost it all. Bad night at the casinos. We tried to make payment arrangements but you don't make arrangements with the mob."

I was listening to his words thinking about Angelo and the Traviano mob family. I may need to call to see if this is something they may know about.

"So you gambled poorly, how does this figure into the theft of a corpse?"

"Well, we couldn't pay back the debt, so they told us we could make up for it by stealing a body from this private morgue. We were given instructions on where to go and what body we needed to take, so Harry and I went there and took the body. Why, I don't know, we were just ordered to do it. We took the corpse and we didn't know where to hide it, so we put it in the freezer in my basement. It was stupid, but it was the only place we could stash it. They told us not to dump the body where it could be found, just to store it."

I was beginning to realize that these lawyers were just stupid and flunkies of a bigger power.

Deacon asked, "So you weren't told why you were supposed to take the body, what about the murder of Spenser, the funeral director?"

"When we were first told our options, they said we could either steal a body or murder a funeral director. We weren't into murder and theft felt less threatening. I figure they found someone else to kill the guy. He was the only funeral director to be murdered lately."

"You have any idea why all this intrigue, what was the motive?"

"I have no idea, we weren't in on that part of the deal. We just did what we did and hoped it would all go away."

"Well, if you had worn gloves to prevent our finding your prints, it might have. Pretty dumb for such smart lawyers. This is telling me nothing, so let's get to the punchline, who ordered your part in this?" Deacon asked.

Thaning looked to Wittly and then quietly said, "Dominic Reslo, he is a front man for the Vespar family in LA. He heads the book runs in Vegas, in charge of the illegal gambling here. He's the money man."

Deacon knew of Reslo, he had been arrested a couple times for numbers and betting under the law. But he was always let off, either through politics or payoffs. "Why would Reslo want Hall's body stolen or Spenser murdered?"

"I have no idea, that's the truth. I just did what I was told."

"Do you know where your partner Harry Brinkley is?"

"Harry works as a investment advisor at a firm on Tropicana out by Rancho Drive. I can give you the address, but I don't know if he's there now. He said he may leave Vegas for a while until this all died down. Bastard left me holding the stiff."

Deacon looked to Morse, "Think that's enough to make a deal?"

Morse smiled and said, "Yeah, I think Mercer has suffered enough. Besides he has to cover his ass now that Reslo is going to be picked up."

Thaning's eyes went wide, "Crap, you said you wouldn't drag my name into this."

Deacon said, "I won't, but it will look like you did rat him out since it's involving you with the body and being arrested. You better think about a new town to live in."

Deacon stood and said Thaning and Wittly could go, but be ready to be questioned again. Deacon went out followed by Morse and they came into observation. I just sat as Deacon plopped down next to me and we watched the two men across the glass huddled, talking quietly.

"Well, I know where Reslo hangs; I'll need you to get an arrest warrant for him, Webb."

The ADA smiled and said he'd have it in an hour and left the room. We continued to watch Thaning and Wittly as they stood and went out of the room, Thaning looking a little pale.

"Okay, why would the Vespar family be interested in Hall's body and the murder of Spenser?" I asked Deacon.

"I guess maybe we'll find out when we bring Reslo in. Maybe. Reslo is a tough nut to crack and he has people in his pocket. We'll be lucky to hold him overnight." He stood and said to go back to Lynn's office.

We went there and Deacon saw Captain Weber coming down the hallway. He stopped and bravely waited for him.

"Got any progress DeAngelo? Hello Richards, are you helping on this?"

I said, "Just working on my case that is linked to the murder of Spenser, Captain."

Deacon spoke quickly, "We have gotten a good lead, Dominic Reslo hired someone to commit the murder and theft of the body Jim was searching for. We found the body and the perp, Mercer Thaning and got Thaning to corroborate the facts on the murder. I'm waiting on the arrest warrant for Reslo to pick him up."

"Good. Very good. You know Reslo has people behind him that will get him out so go into this carefully and cover all the bases. Good work DeAngelo," he said then walked off.

"One good thing about the Captain, he's not long winded. He let's you know what he thinks, then goes away," Deacon said.

"Yep, he's a peach." I went into Lynn's office followed by Deacon and we sat.

Deacon's cell phone rang and he looked to the caller ID, then said to me, "Joe Lang," then answered.

"Yeah Joe, what do you have for me?" He listened for a bit then hung up. "He thawed out Hall and did some more exploring of the body and found a small puncture wound at the base of his spine. Joe said it looked like a large needle mark. The body didn't heal the hole up, since Hall was dead. Joe said he's embarrassed that he missed it. He's changed his cause of death, Hall was murdered."

**

Chapter 13

"That should make the widow Hall very happy, it may fall under accidental death clause and increase his life insurance payout," Deacon said. "Could be a happy twist for her, maybe that's why she wanted Lang to find cause of his death to be murder. She seemed to be the greedy type."

"At last we know now she didn't do it. If Hall was hit with a hypo, it had to be at the banquet. Just before he took a dive into the dip," I said. "I'm surprised he didn't feel it and call for help or at least grab the person who stuck him in the back. I certainly would have clocked any person sticking my backside."

"I wonder if the banquet room had surveillance cameras we can look at. May help, I'll check on it."

Warren came in the doorway with a paper, "Courier just delivered this, your warrant. Do you want me to assemble a team to go get Reslo, he's a tough cookie."

"Thanks Greg it may help, go ahead, just a minimal team."

"Got it," he said and left.

"Shall we rock and roll?" Deacon said. We left the building and he took an unmarked cruiser from the motor pool as the men were gathering in the parking lot. Deacon pulled up and gave directions to the social club where Reslo hung out.

Deacon drove out Flamingo just past Decatur Boulevard and into the parking lot of the building that held the Italian social club. The rest of the cars pulled in, four in total, Warren led the charge of the men following Deacon, I brought up the rear per Deacon's request. Deacon sent three men around back to watch the exits there. Everyone else went into the club and in the near dark, we could see about ten men sitting in various areas of the room, playing cards or just relaxing.

Deacon went to a couple men at the bar and said, "Tell Reslo we need his presence, or we'll tear the place apart to find him."

One of the men stood giving Deacon a hard stare, but Deacon doesn't intimidate easily, he just stared back. "You want to do what I say or shall we take you in for obstructing an arrest warrant?"

The man flinched and went to a door, opened it as Deacon and the cops followed. They went down a hallway to another door. The man opened the door as Deacon pulled him back and went in. It was a small office and the room filled fast with the police as Deacon went to Reslo sitting behind a desk, talking to some greasy looking man sitting in front of the messy desk.

"Dominic Reslo, stand; you are under arrest for conspiracy to commit murder and theft of a corpse," Deacon ordered Reslo as he looked annoyed, then stood slowly. Deacon had Warren cuff him and turn him over to the uniforms. They took him out to the cars quickly.

"Gee, I'm disappointed, he didn't give us a hard time," Warren said. "I was hoping for a shootout."

We walked back through the club as we heard gunshots out front. Everyone ran for the front door and carefully came out into the bright Vegas sunlight. Deacon had his weapon out and was looking around to see what was happening. He went around the side of the building to the parking lot and saw Reslo was on the ground bleeding. The three cops who took him out of the building were trying to keep him alive as they called for an EMS.

"What the hell happened?" Deacon yelled to one of the men.

"We came around the corner of the building just as rifle fire broke out, three quick shots to his chest. We tried to return fire but couldn't locate the shooter. He must have been on top of one of those buildings over there," he said and pointed to a group of buildings housing stores. "It's the only place the shooter could have been, they had to know we were coming, and Reslo was the only one shot. Had to be a hitman."

Deacon ordered the rest of his men to go find the shooter, they all ran off to the buildings in question. Deacon stood looking down at the body of Reslo as he heard the sirens of the EMS in the background.

He looked to me and said, "Warren got his wish, we had a shootout, and Reslo lost the battle."

"Someone didn't want him talking, you have a leak in the department or Wittly and Thaning gave someone a heads up on our coming to get Reslo. This happened all too fast," I said.

"I'm putting my money on Thaning, he probably was covering his ass with the mob," Deacon said as the EMS pulled off the street into the lot. The medical techs jumped out and over to Reslo, and after trying to see if there was any hope for him, they pronounced him dead.

Deacon turned to see the small crowd from the club gathering at the edge of the lot. Deacon saw the man who led us to Reslo and went to him. He got in the guy's face and said, "Are you Reslo's lieutenant?"

The man gave him the same stare as before, Deacon yelled for one of the returning cops and said to take him in for questioning. The cop took the man to a car and put him in the back.

Deacon turned to the other men standing and said, "Any of you people know who may want Reslo dead?"

He got no reply. "Loyalty to the mob is admirable, but it got Reslo killed. Anyone have any ideas why?"

Still no answer. Deacon saw the greasy man from Reslo's office was acting strange, looking around, like he was waiting for another shooter. Deacon went to him, before he saw him and grabbed his coat. "How about you, got anything for me?"

The man was getting a nervous twitch and Deacon called another cop to take him in for questioning also. The officer put him in another car and they drove off.

Deacon watched the rest of the people, now going back into the club. I came up to him and said, "They aren't going to talk are they?"

"Probably not, they are all afraid of what may happen if they do. Reslo didn't even have any warning. Now we are back to square one, but I'm going to run my fist down Thanings throat to see how deep it goes," Deacon said and stormed back to his car. I had to rush to keep up.

We arrived back to the precinct as the uniformed officers were escorting the two men to interrogation. Deacon said to put them in separate rooms. We went in and Williams came up and said his paper trail on the funeral home's unsatisfied customers went nowhere. Deacon asked if Weber was skulking around the building, Williams said he had to go to another briefing for the Secret Service about the presidential visit.

Deacon let out a breath and we went to Lynn's office. Deacon was saying not to sit just as a man came to the door. Deacon asked, "May I help you?"

"Detective DeAngelo?" the man asked.

"The one and only, you are?"

"Special agent Ross Carlton, FBI. I understand you were present during the hit of Dominic Reslo?"

Deacon looked to me with an exasperated expression, "Any more surprises today? Yes Agent Carlton, we were, and just how did you find out so quickly?"

"My confidential informant called to say you had him in custody?"

"I don't have anyone in custody, we have two people in for questioning, is your informant the greasy guy?"

Agent Carlton chuckled to himself and said, "That's one way to describe him, yes, his name is Rico Salvatore and he has been inside the Vespar family for the last year. He was helping us to bring Palo Vesper down by supplying us with intel on the dealings of the family in Vegas, but his information led to bigger fish."

Deacon asked the agent to sit, he did then continued, "The hit on Reslo was something that doesn't surprise me or my office. He's been playing both sides of two different factions in Vegas. One, the Vespar mob and two, a terror cell just forming from out of Afganistan. We were getting close to finding out Reslo's plan when you showed up and tipped someone's hand."

"We have an ongoing murder investigation and Reslo was connected to it. We were going to bring him in for questioning and nail him on murder charges."

"I understand your case, but Reslo was not good at tying up loose ends. Which I think was the reason for his hit. Can we cooperate on our information and get on with the bigger picture?"

"And what would that bigger picture be in regards to Reslo and the Vesper family?"

"Nothing to do with the Vespar family, it involved Reslo and the terrorists who are plotting a major hit on American soil, one that will shake the free world if we let them."

"I don't suppose you can share this with a simple Detective Sergeant and a private investigator?"

He looked to us and said, "You won't divulge this to anyone, it's classified, but to keep you from mucking up our investigation, I'll fill you in, however slightly."

"Well, I wouldn't want to muck up any federal investigation, so yes, please tell us," Deacon said sounding a little annoyed.

"We are investigating intelligence that there will be an assassination attempt on the President of the United States here in Vegas next week."

**

Chapter 14

Trapper told Detective Peters he was done with detecting and needed to go rescue his girlfriend. Peters said he was finished for now with the murder case but would be out later to talk again with Mrs. Walters. Trapper went to his Jeep and drove out to the clinic nestled in the tall Colorado pines out in the country. It was secluded and quiet where the building complex resided and there was a tranquil feeling to the place. Good for recuperating from surgery.

Trapper parked and went to the room where Sam's brother Philip, soon to be Phyllis, was in. He entered the room finding Sam sitting next to an empty bed.

"Where's your brother… I mean sister?" Trapper asked.

"She's having tests done, so they cover all bases.

How did your interrogation go?"

Trapper noticed that Sam had said she, he presumed Sam was getting used to the change. He went to her, giving her a lingering kiss and sat in the chair next to her. He got comfortable and took Sam's hand.

"Well, we know the fiancé didn't do it. It's a long story, so I'll tell you later. How are you feeling?"

"Well, this is all so strange; I'm losing a brother and gaining a sister. We talked all while you were gone and got a lot of baggage out in the open. I now understand what he is going through, the doctors also explained a good deal about it to me. Seems it's more common than people realize. There's a lot more transgendered people out there in hiding. It's a shame we can't be more tolerant of the differences in people."

They sat holding hands, talking, just as Phillip was wheeled back in and put in the bed. Trapper greeted him and asked how he felt.

"Like a person who is being reborn, and not in a religious sense. I'm anxious but apprehensive at the same time. I've wanted this for years and now it's happening, it's scary."

They talked a bit more about the procedure then Phillip asked them to leave, he wanted to get some sleep. Trapper and Sam left the room and went back to Trapper's car. They stopped at a Burger King and ate a late lunch and then drove back to the Bed and Breakfast.

Mrs. Walters greeted them from her chair behind the desk, "How are you kids doing today?"

"Well, considering all the excitement from yesterday, we're holding up well," Sam offered.

"You may like to know that Terrence Rice didn't murder his fiancé, he had a good alibi. Has he come back yet?" Trapper said.

"I haven't seen him," she replied.

Trapper thought that was odd, Rice was released and supposedly brought back here. He thought he'd wait before he called Peters over something trivial.

They talked a little more about the weather and then Trapper and Sam went up to their room passing the door with the yellow crime tape across it.

~~*~~

Deacon and I just sat stunned by the revelation of a presidential assassination, Deacon spoke first, "Why don't they just tell the president to stay home and that will end it?"

"Not that simple, we need to catch these people and Rico says that Reslo was bragging about a bigger attack on Vegas if they failed to get the president, it was mentioned that there was a dirty bomb involved. We are treading on thin ice trying to weigh the options."

Dirty bomb, I thought about the virus attack I almost stopped last month, now someone wants to destroy Vegas with a dirty bomb. Maybe I should move Penny and I back to Michigan. This town was getting too dangerous.

"So are you going to parade the president out to be killed or what?" I asked.

Carlton smiled, "No, we wouldn't do that and the Secret Service won't let us. We're playing up to the day and hopefully we can find them before they strike."

"So what do you know so far and how does it fit in with our murders?"

"As far as our investigation goes, your dead men had something to do with the possible shutdown of the hotels around Vegas. If Hall had called for a strike that would have caused the unions to walk out, basically shutting down the city and the president probably would have changed his plans. The terrorists didn't want anything to get in the way of their plans so Hall and Spenser were expendable."

"I'd like to close my case by arresting someone, any chance of that happening?" Deacon asked.

"I don't know who Reslo hired to do the hit on Spenser or Hall. I do know he was brought in from out of town according to Rico, and he's probably left town now that his job is finished."

"Who hit Reslo?" I asked.

"That was probably set up by the Vespar family. Reslo, as I said, burned his candle at both ends and was not too careful about it. Palo Vespar demanded total loyalty from his people; Reslo didn't give him the respect. So we figure he was set-up for the hit and it just happened when you showed up to arrest him."

"How did you know we had Rico in custody?" Deacon asked.

"He called me on his cell phone when your men put him in the patrol car. I came quickly to head off any problems."

I was sure Deacon felt a bit dumb on that question, everyone had cell phones now days, even gang bangers.

Deacon called out to Warren, he came in. "Cut the fat guy loose and keep the greasy guy, we're not done with him."

Warren went off and then we saw him escorting the guy out. Deacon stood and said, "I'd like to talk with Rico, to tie up my loose ends."

Carlton said that was fine with him, and then we all went to interrogation and into where Rico was sitting, looking nervous. He saw Carlton and got a big smile on his face.

"Hey Agent Carlton, you got here okay?" he spoke with a quaver in his voice; I figured this guy either had a nervous condition or a drinking problem.

"Yes Rico, I take care of my people. Now Detective DeAngelo would like to ask you a few questions to tie up his murder case, tell him what you know, all right?"

"Sure, it's okay by me. What you want to know detective?"

Deacon sat as we followed his lead. We got comfortable as Deacon waited for the room to quiet. He leaned over the table and said, "You're an informant for the FBI, correct?"

Rico looked to Carlton, who nodded to him, and then Rico said, "Yep, I am. I can tell you all I know about the mob people I'm involved with. Ask anything of me, I got the inside track."

"I'm interested in who killed Spenser the funeral director, and the union rep Hall. What do you know about that?"

Rico paused like he was pulling things from his memory banks, he made a number of pained expressions, probably having brain farts.

"I know Reslo called in some jamoke from out east, New Jersey I think. Dominic called him Spider, I don't think that was his real name so you figure it out. He wasn't very bright but he was a real good killer I heard. I know Spider left town after the hits and Dominic paid him off."

I now knew I would definitely call Angelo out in New York to see if his mob connections could find this Spider.

"How did you figure into Reslo's posse?" Deacon asked.

"What? What's that mean?"

"How were you hooked into Reslo, why were you in his confidence?"

"Oh, I see, yeah, I was Reslo's monkey, I kept him amused and he let me hang around him. He didn't think I was any threat. Too bad he didn't know I was a snitch for the Feds." He sat back chuckling and gave us a badly toothy smile, dirty teeth and in need of a dentist. The teeth fit in with his greasy look, slicked back hair and pointy nose reminding me of a weasel. Which he was.

"Do you know anything about the assassination attempt..." Deacon was abruptly cut off by Carlton.

"I'm sorry Detective but that is part of my investigation and not to be discussed by anyone but me and my CI. Right Rico?"

"You got it boss, I'm your CI."

I wondered if he even knew what CI meant. Deacon stood and thanked Rico and Carlton and said they could both leave now. Carlton stood and motioned to Rico to get up and follow. We all went out of the interrogation room and Deacon thanked the men for their cooperation. They responded and left.

After they were out of the squad room, Deacon turned to me and said, "I'm not sure why, but I don't care much for either of them. Do you have the same opinion?"

"Well, Rico I can understand, he's just a low life creep. Carlton, I have a feeling has an agenda, either he's on the up and up or he's plotting something. I just watched his expressions as he talked to you; he seems to be hiding something."

"Glad we are on the same track, I'm going to call in a few markers with my friends in the FBI and get an opinion of Carlton."

"Good, I'm going to call my mob connections and see if I can track down Spider for you."

"Are you referring to Angelo? Your mob enforcer buddy?"

"One and the same. If anyone knows what is going on in the underworld, Angelo will."

**

Chapter 15

I first met Angelo when Penny and I came to Las Vegas from Michigan to get married about a year and a half ago. That's when we got involved in the Bridezilla murders, and the mob enforcer Angelo was in town with the Traviano Family wedding. His mother, Francis, was marrying don Gino Traviano when she was grabbed by the Bridzilla killer, we saved her. The Traviano's were thankful and I became a friend.

I sat in Lynn's office with Deacon as he was on the phone with his friends in the FBI. I decided to call Penny before calling Angelo to see how she was doing, she came on after two rings, "Pervert's Delight, may I entice you into a fantasy," She answered.

I was not surprised by this; she had a strange sense of humor that I loved. "Do you have a fantasy involving a threesome?"

"You keep bringing that up! I said you, me and the blow-up doll can do it, but that's as far as I go."

"Spoil sport. Where are you and what are you doing?"

"I'm at home, I stopped at the office but Lacey said you were off chasing killers. She also told me to warn you to stop scaring her with your ghost moves of popping out on her. Are you coming home soon, I'd like to go out to eat, and at a decent restaurant, no burger joints."

"Hey, I don't deliberately try to scare Lacey, she just lives in her own little world and isn't aware of her surroundings. I'll try to be more caring about jumping out at her. Yes, I'll be home soon and we can go eat out. Later I need to call Angelo out in New York about the case I'm helping Deacon on."

"Angelo? Sounds important. I'd like to talk to Francis to see how she's doing."

"Great, give me about an hour and be ready to go eat," I said and hung up.

Deacon finished with his call as I watched him. "My contacts in the bureau say Carlton's a good guy, no blemishes on his record. Maybe I just misread him. Well, what shall we do now?"

"I'm leaving you, going home to kiss my wife and take her to an expensive dinner. You can go home and open a can of beans," I said with a smile.

"How did you know what I had planned?"

"I'm psychic, so I shall depart you, see you in the morning and hopefully I'll have something from Angelo." I stood, saluted him and went out to my car.

~~*~~

Trapper and Sam were resting on the bed when they heard a knock at the door. It was Scott Peters.

"Hey Scott, what's up?" Trapper said.

"You haven't seen Terrence Rice have you?" he asked.

"No, we got back here and Mrs. Walters said he hadn't returned. We've been in here resting for the last hour or so. He's not in the extra room Mrs.

Walters set up for him, since his room is a crime scene now?"

"No, and she says she didn't see him returned. I'm wondering if he may be involved in the murder now and skipped town."

"You think he spent time in the bar to provide an alibi?"

"I'm thinking that, but I don't know why he would murder Foster. Was his relationship that bad?"

"I don't know, have you checked in his room, maybe he's asleep?"

"I banged on the door enough to wake him, but I may have Mrs. Walter open up his room to see if his belongings are there. Thanks." He went back down the hall and Trapper closed the door.

Trapper asked Sam if she was hungry. She got up from the bed and said, "I thought you'd never ask. Let me freshen up and we can go to that same place we were at last night, I liked the food." She went to the bathroom and closed the door. Trapper changed his shirt and looked at himself in the dresser mirror, "You are a handsome devil."

Sam came out and asked, "Are you talking to yourself?"

"Just admiring my reflection."

She went to the mirror, looked closely, "Nope no cracks, I guess you passed the mirror test."

Trapper smacked her behind and they kissed. "This won't get you out of paying for the meal tonight," She said.

They went to the door and out into the hallway to find Peters and Mrs. Walters at Rice's door. She was just opening it up as they came by. Peters pulled Mrs. Walters back carefully as he went into the room. Trapper stopped Sam and watched what was going on as they heard Peters quietly say "Damn" but loud enough for Trapper to hear.

He went to the door and looked in. Rice was on the floor with blood pooled around him and a knife in his hand. Peters looked to Trapper and said, "Sort of looks like he took his own life, doesn't it?"

"Without further examination, I'd say that also."

~~*~~

Penny and I decided to try a new restaurant south on the strip. It was a nice looking place from outside, but the inside was plush and expensive looking. Lots of red velvet curtains and plush dark purple carpeting. The hostess was in an evening gown, I suddenly felt underdressed. She smiled and suddenly looked shocked, I was waiting for it.

"Oh my, you're Penny Wickens!" There it was. Penny smiled and said she was, and the hostess took us to a table right up front, where everyone could see us. She left the menus and told us she'd be right back.

"I get the feeling we are being put on display," I said as I looked around the semi dark room, watching the other diners watching us.

A few beats later and man in a tuxedo approached and said, "Good evening, I'm Vincent Kerr, the owner and I'd like to say that I'm pleased that you and your famous detective husband have joined us tonight, Mrs. Wickens."

Penny went to correct him, but I held up my hand and said to let it go. He said, "I'd like to send a bottle of champagne to your table, on the house."

Penny said, "Well thank you that would be fine." He beamed and skittered off.

"I'll have to take you to new restaurants more often, Mrs. Wickens," I said.

A waiter came by with champagne in a silver pail and sat two glasses in front of us. He asked if he could pour, I said it would be fine. He popped the plastic stopper and poured the liquid out and we sipped the drink. I said it was very good, he smiled and said he'd be back for our order.

"So what have you accomplished today?" Penny asked.

"We found the body of John Hall and identified the killer, which is why I have to call Angelo, the killer was mob connected. Not to the Traviano family, but from that area."

"So Hall was murdered, did Joe Lang confirm this?"

"Yep, he found a needle mark on the back end of Hall's body and we found an FBI snitch who confirmed the kill."

"FBI? You really are getting in deep aren't you?"

"You know I always do, if it's murder, I have cops around me."

"Good, they can help keep you alive," Penny said with a smile.

"I'm capable of taking care of myself," I defended.

"You can't get out of bed without me pushing you. If I wasn't around you'd fall apart."

"Okay, I agree with that, but when it comes to crime, I'm good."

"Don't strain yourself with that arm slapping your back," she said then picked up her menu and covered her face, but I could tell she was laughing.

Our dinner was superb, and the service was fantastic. I wondered if ordinary people got this treatment, but what the hell, I enjoyed it. We paid, tipped everyone and thanked the owner for a wonderful experience. He said to be sure to return and we went out to my car being brought up by the valet.

We pulled back into the drive at home and into the garage. I opened the door to the house and Willy came flying out at us. I figured he was mad for leaving him alone, so I went to get him some food. Penny said she was taking a dip in the pool, I said I was calling Angelo. I said I would come out by the pool to call so she could talk to Francis.

She was out and in the water as I came out and sat on one of the plastic lawn chairs. I went through the phone book on my Palm Treo cell phone and pulled out Angelo's number. I pushed the button to auto-dial and waited.

After a few rings the phone was answered, "Yeah, Angelo here, who's dis?"

"Angelo, Jim Richards here," I said.

"Hey Mr. Richards, good to hear from youse."

I see his speech hadn't changed, I love listening to him, he sounded like one of those gangsters in the old movies.

"Angelo, I'm not disturbing anything?"

"Nah, I'm just shootin pool wit some buddies. Wotcha need?"

"I have a question that maybe you can help me with? I'm looking for a hitman you may know or can help me find."

"You looking to hire a hitman, I know a few I could send out, who ya gonna kill?"

"No my friend, I'm trying to find a hitman who murdered a couple good people out here. I'm told he came in from New Jersey."

"Wot's his moniker? I know a couple mugs from Joisy."

"I don't have his name but he goes by the nickname Spider."

Angelo was quiet for a beat, and then said, "Ya, I know da creep, ya want him whacked, I'll take care of it for youse."

I just laughed and said that wouldn't be necessary.

**

Chapter 16

Trapper and Sam stood off the side of the hall watching the same police crew that was there yesterday, back again. Peters came up and said, "The

ME says it looks like a suicide, but he'll know more when he gets the body to the morgue. He stabbed himself up through the heart; ME said it was a quick death. I just can't figure out people sometimes, makes my job all that harder." He shook his head and went back to the room.

Trapper took Sam down the stairs and came to the desk where Mrs. Walters was looking surprisingly calm. "Mrs. Walters, are you all right?" Sam asked.

She jerked her head a bit as if she was pulled out of a daydream and smiled, "I'm fine dear, it's just been a rough two days, what with the deaths. I just may want to sell the place; it's been such a chore since my husband died last year."

"Well, I'm sure you'll do the right thing. We're going to go eat now, we'll be back late, so don't wait up for us," Sam said with a smile.

Mrs. Walters said to enjoy and then she drifted back off into her own little world.

Trapper and Sam left the building going past the police guarding the front entrance, avoiding all the press people who were now gathering out front, refusing comment as they rush the couple. They walked the short distance to the restaurant and went in.

Mrs. Walters was now rocking and smiling, staring at the box of knives she had under the counter.

~~*~~

"No Angelo, I want to see him brought to justice, and my police friend Deacon would like to nab him for the murders. So if you can just locate him and let me know, Deacon can get hold of the Jersey police and extradite him back here."

"Seems ta me my idea would be faster." Angelo laughed. I figured he was kidding me when he mentioned about whacking Spider. Angelo had a good sense of humor about his role as a mob wiseguy. He liked to yank my chain about it when he could.

"Yes, I agree, but Deacon has a sense of duty to the law, so if you can just find him and let me know, I'd appreciate it."

"Sure will, Mr. R. and I'll see dat he doesn't go on da run."

"Thanks Angelo, now is your mother around? Penny would like to say hi."

"She sure is, she's racking the billiard balls now, I'll get her." He put the phone down and I handed my cell to Penny who had gotten out of the pool when she saw me talking.

Penny held the phone for a moment then brightened when Francis came on. They talked for about twenty minutes, mostly Penny talking about moving to Vegas. Then she listened to Francis talking and then they said good-byes and Penny hung up handing my phone back to me.

"That was so nice to talk to her; she says she misses my show since I quit the national telecast. She asked me to send tapes of my show here so she can see how it looks. I'll talk to Gordy and get some tapes to send."

Penny reached out her hand to me, I took it as she said, "Want to go get naked and roll around the bed for a while? You can play the mob wiseguy and I'll be the moll."

"Can we include the blow-up doll?"

She let go of my hand and stood, "I'll be in the bedroom, alone." Then she went off, leaving me with Willy staring at me.

"You're on your own pal, I'm going to get some, and don't tear the house apart." I went in followed by the pup, down the hall into the bedroom and closed the door, leaving him in the hallway. He gave a snort, curled up on the rug and closed his eyes.

About two hours later, after some fooling around and some rest we were on the couch in the living room watching a comedy on the TV when my cell phone rang, the caller ID said it was Deacon. I went to the kitchen so not to disturb Penny and answered.

"What's up chief?" I said.

"Did you talk to Angelo?" he asked.

"Yep, he knows Spider and will get his location and let me know. I had to stop him from wanting to whack Spider but maybe I should let him." I smiled as I heard Deacon laugh.

"No, I would like to get him back here to find out what he knows about this mess. You think it will take too much time to get hold of him? I can call a friend in the Trenton police to run interference for me."

"Let's just see what Angelo comes up with first before we send your posse on a chase for someone we don't have yet."

"Good idea, don't want the east coast law enforcement mad at me. They probably couldn't find him any faster than the mob can anyways. You still coming in tomorrow morning?"

"I'll be in after I crawl out of bed, so start the day without me and I'll see you later." I laughed and hung up.

Penny and I watched a little more television then went into the bedroom to sleep.

~~*~~

Trapper and Sam arrived back at the North Denver Bed and Breakfast around 11:30 and didn't see Mrs. Walters behind the desk. They went quietly up to their room to go to bed. Philip's surgery was scheduled for tomorrow around 11 AM and Sam wanted to be there for him.

They were quickly undressed and in bed, Sam saying she wanted to just sleep. Trapper grumbled about having to wait, but he laid back and soon they both were asleep. Sam was a heavy sleeper; Trapper was the kind of person who drifted in and out. He was in the middle of a drift inward when he thought he heard a noise at the door. He stayed still listening and then thought nothing of it. He turned on his side facing the wall when he heard the noise by the bed; he turned barely able to see in the dark room, as the figure raised an arm poised to strike down at Sam with what looked like a knife.

Trapper grabbed his pillow and threw it at the figure if only to distract. He turned and reached to the shoulder holster draped over the chair next to him and pulled his Sig Sauer out and came back over ready to fire, but the figure was gone. He looked to the door, which was open slightly and got out of bed racing to the door. He burst out of the room and looked both ways. He stood still listening for any noise; he heard a movement in the next room. He knew it was not supposed to be occupied and went there.

He put his ear close to the door, listened and heard a movement. He tried the door handle and it was locked, so he reared up with his foot and smashed the door in. He held his weapon out and then carefully moved into the opening. The house was old so there were no light switches at the door but the light from the hallway provided enough light to see in the room.

He moved to a lamp on a table and switched it on, lighting the room to which he found empty. He turned to the bathroom door, which was slightly ajar and pushed it open with his hand. He entered and slowly went to the center of the room just as the bathtub curtain flew open and the figure lashed out with the knife. Trapper did a spin to avoid the blade, spun completely around and came back facing the attacker. He was shocked to see it was a man with a badly scarred face.

He brought the gun up and yelled for him to stop, but he came at him. He didn't want to fire on him so he gave him a good smash to the face with his free fist sending him falling back into the tub. He lay there not moving. Trapper reached down to feel the pulse in his neck as the man came up with his arm and made contact with the knife to Trapper's side. He roared in pain, brought the gun up and fired directly at the man. He jerked a couple times in the tub and was staring at the ceiling now, not moving, bleeding out.

Trapper yelled for Sam, who heard the gun shot and she came running into the room. "Go call the police, quckly!" She saw the body in the tub and ran back out, down the stairs and to the phone at the desk.

As she was just connecting with 911, she felt her hair being grabbed and she was jerked back from the desk. Sam wasn't a light weight, she had to be tough when she was a madam for the escort service, so she grabbed back and made connection with the arm, twisting it and spun herself and the assailant around pushing the person to the wall. She pinned the arm back and then realized it was Mrs. Walters. She didn't care, and held on as she yelled for Trapper. He came out of the door, to the top of the stairs and saw what was going on. He flew down the stairs, took hold of the woman and pushed her to the rocking chair.

"What's going on?!" he yelled, "and who is the person I shot upstairs?"

The old woman's eyes went big, "You shot him, oh God, no! Is he alive?"

"Barely, I need the police." He went to the phone and found it still connected to 911. He explained what he needed, an EMS and Detective Peters, ASAP.

**

Chapter 17

I woke early and went to the kitchen to find Willy had dragged his bag of dry food around the kitchen, leaving small pellets of food all over the floor. I looked to him sitting in the middle of the mess as he just stared up with his dumb cute expression. I knew we weren't giving him a lot of attention so he was lashing out. I got the broom out and started cleaning up the mess.

Penny came out as I was sweeping and asked me if I had an accident.

"Not with the dog kibble, Willy decided to decorate the kitchen. I think he needs attention. Can you start taking him with you to the studio a couple times a week, he probably thinks Lacey is his owner since we dump him there most the time."

"I'll take the poor baby with me today," she said as she picked the pup up and snuggled him. I finished cleaning and went to my bathroom to get ready for the day.

An hour later, we both were ready to go out in the world and kissed at the door as we went to our cars and drove into our jobs. I went by the office first before bothering Deacon and came in the back door of the building. As I was coming down the hallway to the front lobby I yelled, "I'm here and I'm entering the front!" I heard a yelp before I got there.

"That's not working either! You scared me by yelling in the hall," Lacey moaned.

"All right I'll start coming in the front door, will that work for you?"

"I think it would."

"I know, I'll put an extra large bell on the back door so you will know when someone comes in. Boy, you are a nervous Nellie."

"A warning from the back would be good. Deacon called to see if you were here. He said he tried your cell phone but got voice mail again."

I was amazed when I found my cell phone was shut off again, I don't remember doing it. I thought that maybe I shut it off in my sleep since it was on the bed table next to me. Maybe I subconsciously did it to avoid being disturbed.

"Thanks, I'll call him now," I said as I went to my office.

He came on and asked right off, "Any word from Angelo?"

"Well, good morning to you too. No, I haven't heard yet since it is only 8:05 in the morning."

"Well it's 11:05 in New York, so they've had time to find him."

"Deacon, he'll call as soon as he gets something, so relax. I know you want to tie this case up but it won't do any good to worry about it. Now, have you heard from Lynn?" I said to change the subject.

"Yeah, she's scheduled to testify tomorrow, if nothing screws up, so she may be back the following day, I hope."

"Good, maybe that will calm you. You really need sex to relax," I said trying not to laugh at his predicament.

"I'm sure that will help. Are you coming in?"

"Do you need me?"

"Not really, I just like your company."

"Well, I have some paperwork to do, billing stuff so I get paid for my efforts. I'll stop in later," I said and we finished the call.

I sat in my office for a couple hours working on the bill for my dead body recovery and goofing around on the computer working on writing my neglected next book when I heard the front door bell tinkle. I waited and then Lacey popped up at my door and said with wide eyes, "You really need to get out here."

I jumped up wondering what horrible thing was in the lobby when I came out to find two huge men on each side of a smaller man holding him in place. Behind the men I heard a familiar voice, "Hey, Mr. R., we poisonally brought ya da Spider. Did we do good?" Then Angelo peeked around the mass of men and smiled.

~~*~~

Detective Peters was stunned to find that Mrs. Walters was involved in the murder of her guests. He had the woman in the sitting room off the lobby, and was talking to her as Trapper stood by. Trapper had called a cab for Sam to go to the clinic and said he'd be out after they were finished.

The EMS had taken out the mystery man; he was still alive but barely. Mrs. Walters was fretting over him and insisting she go with the man, but Peters insisted that she stay.

"Mrs. Walters, who is that man?" he asked as he sat on a foot stool in front of the woman.

She was silent for a moment then spoke, "He's my son, I've kept him hidden for so long after his accident in the explosion where everyone thought he was killed."

Peters was shocked to remember an incident three years ago when the police were chasing the man they called the Denver Slasher and he went in to a building that he had wired to explode. They had thought he was killed.

"How did he survive?"

"He had a tunnel going out of the building, but he was caught in the explosion just as he got in the tunnel and was badly burned. He did get out and I took care of him, I used to be a registered nurse years ago. I kept him safely in my basement since then. My husband was against it and my son, Marty was his name, fixed my husband's car so it would crash, killing him. I loved my son so dearly, I couldn't turn him over to the police. I never cared much for my husband, so it was a welcome relief to be rid of him," she said and went silent.

"Your son was a murderer; didn't that make you want to turn him in?" Peters asked.

"He was my son, I loved him," she said with tears in her eyes.

Peters looked over to Trapper, sighed and stood

113

going to Trapper, "Well, it explains a few things. We'll take her in and talk more to her. Thanks for wrapping this up."

Trapper smiled, "We were lucky, he almost got us too."

Peters had his men take Mrs. Walters to the precinct and asked Trapper to lock up the house when they were done and said, "This is going to be hard to explain to my mother, they were friends. Crazy world huh?"

~~*~~

"How did you get here so fast?" I yelled to Angelo over the mountain of men.

He came around to me and said, "We got holda Spider last night, den we took Gino's private jet ta get here."

"Must be nice to have a private jet. You didn't kidnap him did you?"

"Nah, he came willingly, didn't ya Spider?" he said to the man. The guy shook his head vigorously with a sickly smile. I can imagine that they convinced him to come with them.

"Fantastic, I'll Call Deacon and have him come to pick Spider up." I turned to Lacey and asked her to call Deacon; she got on the phone and called him. I went back to my desk drawer and took out the handcuffs I had there and brought them back to cuff Spider to the arm of the couch. The two gigantic men left the building, got in a black limo parked out front and it drove off.

114

I asked Angelo where they were going.

"Back to da hotel, we got rooms before coming here."

I shook Angelo's hand and said, "It's so good to see you again. How's Gino and Francis?"

"They're good. Mom came with us, she's in da hotel spa getting ready to go out on the town."

I smiled at the thought of the woman in her late seventies partying in Vegas. "I'll call Penny and let her know. What hotel are you at?"

"The Tropicana again, mom feels comfortable there."

"I'll tell Penny and she can meet her after her show."

Lacey interrupted and said, "Deacon is coming over with his men, he said he was overjoyed, his own words, that we got him, meaning Spider."

I thanked her and took Angelo to the other couch in the lobby and we sat. "So tell me how you found our friend here?" I said looking to Spider as he sat quietly on his couch.

"I called a few people I knew and they put me on him, luckily he was in New York on business and we found him. We talked him into coming back with us and here we are."

I noticed his speech pattern was better, maybe he liked pulling my leg with the gangster talk. He continued, "We brought him back to the compound and I asked Gino if we could use the jet to bring him here for ya. Gino said he was glad ta help and get da murderous scum out of New York. Mom thought it would be a great vacation and came along. So here we are."

"Well, this is great, now we can have a good time in Vegas, after we get Spider to Deacon."

"Yeah, I'd like ta see a big number show, lots of music and singing. Plus I'd like to see the new Sinatra Restaurant."

I had read about the restaurant and said, "Anywhere you want to go for all the trouble you went to on this."

"It was no trouble at all, Spider here was more than anxious to come back to Vegas, weren't ya Spider?"

The man just stared at Angelo with his sickly smile and nodded his head.

**

Chapter 18

Deacon came flying in followed by three uniformed officers. He was grinning like a goofy kid on Christmas day, he really needed sex.

"Angelo, thank you so much for bringing Spider back for us," he said as he instructed the officers to take the hitman back to the station. I unlocked the cuffs and they read him his rights, replaced the cuffs with their own, and dragged the man out to the waiting patrol car.

"So how did you find him?" Deacon asked Angelo, even though I could tell he wanted to go interrogate Spider.

"Why don't I tell you about that later, you probably need to talk to your suspect while he still is willing to talk," I said.

"Yeah, that's true, I'll talk to you later. Thanks again Angelo," he said and rushed out the door to his car.

"He's a nervous one," Angelo said with a grin.

"He's under a lot of pressure with the murder and his girlfriend is out of town, so his sex life is suffering."

"Hey, this town is fulla hookers, he should indulge," Angelo said.

"I told him that, but he's faithful. Now my friend, shall we go see your mother and I'll call Penny, then we can all go out to eat. I'll get us into Sinatra's."

We got up and I went into my office after excusing myself and called Penny. "You'll never guess who I have in my office?" I said when she answered.

"Cher? Celine Dion? How would I know, I'm not a mentalist," she protested.

"Angelo."

"What! Is Francis there too?"

"No, but she's at the Tropicana having a spa treatment and I'm going to take Angelo there. Do you want to meet us and go for food at Sinatra's?"

"I'm on my way, I'm just having my show make-up removed."

"Have your girls put on the Angelina Jolie face."

She was quiet for a bit then said, "Only if you can look like Brad Pitt," she said, then hung up laughing.

Mortuary Murders

I went back out to the lobby, told Lacey to hold my calls and took Angelo out to my car.

~~*~~

Trapper was in the Denver PD precinct waiting for Scott Peters to finish talking with Mrs. Walters. He had called Sam and told her what was going on and that he would be out shortly. Sam said Philip was in surgery and it would take about eight to ten hours, so she was bored. Trapper said he'd bring her some magazines.

Peters came up to Trapper in the squad room and sat on the chair next to him. "I'm amazed. I just found out that one of Denver's most notorious serial killers was the son of my mother's friend. Walters had harbored him all these years after the explosion that we thought ended his terror reign. He was scarred so badly and along with his mental state, she kept him hidden away. We also solved a number of missing person reports; they all were murdered at the bed and breakfast and buried in the back yard. Walters is a little imbalanced herself but being cooperative. You just don't really know people."

"Welcome to the real world. Are you all finished with me, I've been poked and probed enough and I want to go to see my girlfriend."

"Will, it's been good to know you, if I don't see you again. We're done, I got your statement and I doubt you'll need to testify, but you never know," he said as he stood.

Trapper stood and they shook hands, then

Trapper left the building and drove to the clinic, but stopping first to buy a bunch of magazines.

~~*~~

I drove us to the Tropicana, parked, went in to find Penny coming into the lobby after we waited for her. She called me to say she was coming as Angelo called his mother and told her we were in the lobby. We found Francis and the four of us went back out and to Sinatra's Restaurant at the Encore Hotel.

We sat at a table as Francis was asking Penny all kinds of questions about her show. I was amazed that this 80-something grand lady of a New York mafia family was excited like any other ordinary everyday woman about a TV show.

"Francis, would you like to come watch my show being recorded tomorrow?" Penny asked.

"Yes dear, I would love that! What time do you want me to be ready?" she replied.

I spoke, "I can come by to pick you up in the limo that you and Gino gave me. Be ready by 8 AM tomorrow morning out front of the Tropicana lobby. Angelo can escort you and come with us."

Angelo beamed, "I'd like to go too, thanks."

We had our excellent food and then left. I drove everyone around Vegas giving the nickel tour then drove to our home. Francis and Angelo were impressed with the view we had of the valley and the strip. We sat out back talking about life in the big city and crime in the east coast of New York. Well, not really talking about crime but Francis filled us in on how Gino and the family were doing. Later, after we finished, Francis, Penny and I went back to the Tropicana in the limo now being driven by Angelo. Francis had few pleasant memories of the car and told us about them.

We dropped them off and arranged to meet in the morning, then Penny and I drove back to the house and in to settle for the night.

~~*~~

Earlier in the day, Deacon had Spider sitting in one of the interrogation rooms and he let the hitman sweat it out. A half hour later, the ADA, Webb Morse, came in to watch the questioning and Deacon said he would get started.

Deacon entered the room slamming the door against the wall as he came in causing Spider to jump in his seat. Deacon planted himself on the chair across from Spider and leaned into him.

"So, in reality you are Horace Worley, you must have been popular when you were a kid. Teased much? I can see that you would take on a life of crime with a handle like that. I hear that you told the Traviano family that you would come in to confess to the murder of John Hall, rep for the Culinary Union and the murder of Michael Spenser, funeral director. Is that correct, Horace?"

Spider sat looking at himself in the mirror. He was in a quandary; if he didn't confess he would incur the wrath of Angelo and his men. If he did confess then the nasty people who hired him would see that he was killed. Either way he was a dead man. May as well take down the nasty men he thought, maybe Angelo would protect him for the good deed.

"Yeah, I did both hits," he finally said.

"Good boy Horace. Now I need to know who hired you and why?"

He sat for a minute putting his thoughts together to see if he could come out of this without the stink from the people who hired him. He looked to Deacon with tired eyes, having not slept well on the jet flight out from New York to Vegas and being dragged around by the wiseguys and police.

"I was brought into town by Dominic Reslo, he said he was hiring me for a group of people who wanted Hall and Spenser out of the way so they could go ahead with their plan." He went silent again.

"What plan?" Deacon demanded loudly.

Spider jumped, and said, "I'm not totally sure, but Reslo was such a putz and he liked bragging on his involvement in the plot to shake up this country. He said that there were people from a foreign country that wanted Hall and Spenser out of the way so they wouldn't prevent their plan to attack the United States from happening."

"I already know about the attack Horace, but who are these people? Give me names."

"Reslo didn't let me in on his confidence; I have no idea who they are." He went silent again. Then he looked to Deacon and said, "Okay, I did hear one name, Fasel Nabib, and Reslo said he was in Vegas to start planning the attack. That's all I heard, honestly."

Deacon was going to ask another question when Ross Carlton, FBI, burst into the room.

"I'm sorry Detective, I was in the observation room watching your questioning and this interview is over. I'm taking this man in as abetting and witness to a terrorist plotting against the United States."

Deacon stood and came between Carlton and Spider and said, "Not on my watch, he's my prisoner."

"Well, Sergeant DeAngelo, I have a little more pull than you do. I'm sorry, but I will take your prisoner to be interrogated by my people."

Captain Weber stepped into the room and he didn't look happy. "Deacon," he said, the first time he ever used Deacon's first name, "As much as I want this man for the murders, I have to insist we turn Worley over to the Feds. It's for the good of the country. Do you understand?"

Deacon looked to the Fed, then to Spider, then to Weber. He wished Jim was there to guide him but he realized he had to grow up and take control of his life. He gave in.

"You better share what you have with us or you can kiss this arrangement good-bye. I have a few connections in the mafia now that you can't control, Agent Carlton. They brought Spider here and they have ways to take him back."

Deacon spoke the words hoping Carlton didn't know the situation and could buy some time for his case.

   **

Chapter 19

I picked up Francis and Angelo at the Tropicana and drove them and Penny towards her studio. Francis insisted that she wanted to hold Willy. She laughed remembering back when we first came to her door in the hotel just before her wedding and kidnap by the Bridezilla killer. We had Willy with us then and she had asked if he was a police dog.

We arrived at the studio, went in and Penny introduced them to Gordy, who remembered the Bridezilla case and their involvement. He was excited to meet real mob figures. Penny went to get ready and took Francis with her, as Angelo and I sat on chairs in the studio where Penny's show was going to be taped.

I excused myself and called Deacon, he came on sounding a little groggy. "Did I wake you?"

"It's okay, I took the day off," he said sounding down.

"What's the matter, what about Spider?" Angelo heard my reference and leaned over to listen. Deacon told me about Carlton taking Spider away and Deacon was fed up with the intrusions.

"I'm going to close the case even though we don't have Spider in custody, and we can't prosecute unless the FBI turns him back to us, and I doubt they will. This sucks."

"Well, you did close the case, you got the killer. It's no different now than if the courts turned him out. The FBI won't go easy on him will they?"

"Yeah, you're right. I guess I was hoping for a total wrap-up on this. I guess I did all I could."

"Yes, my friend, you did. Now relax and go find a hooker," I said with a laugh.

"Lynn called last night and is going to be back tomorrow, so I'm taking a short leave from work to spend time with her."

"Yeah, I know what kind of time you two will spend. Talk later," I said and hung up.

I turned to Angelo and explained the whole situation to him. He wasn't happy that the Feds had stuck their noses into it but he was pleased that he could help.

We watched Penny's show being taped, she had a couple local entertainers on that had some notoriety and she had a portion of a production from one of the musicals going on in town. They wrapped the show and Penny went to get her TV make-up changed back to her street face.

We left the studio and went for lunch at Bistros, ate and then I took Penny to get her car at the studio that she left there yesterday, and I drove Angelo and Francis back to our home to relax.

Around 4:30, Deacon was still lounging in bed in his apartment when the phone call came; it was Warren. "Hey Deacon, sorry to interrupt your day off but I just wanted to let you know some scuttlebutt I heard from my friends in the bureau, seems your man Horace Worley turned up dead this morning. FBI is looking into how it happened and they're baffled. He was murdered in his cell and there's no evidence that anyone got close to him."

"How was he killed?" Deacon asked as he got up from the bed.

"Well, details are sketchy but I hear he was poisoned, just like he did to John Hall the union rep. Looks like someone didn't want him to talk to the Feds."

"Thanks Greg, appreciate the info." They finished and he hung up. "Crap, this just gets deeper all the time," he said to himself.

My cell phone rang shortly after Deacon took his call, I answered. "Are you tired of doing nothing already?" I said.

"Spider was murdered this morning," was all he said.

"How and was he in custody with the Feds?"

"He was poisoned in his cell in the FBI building in town. Someone is still putting roadblocks up. I'm going to go into the station to find out more, ask Angelo if he can find out anything. Thanks," he said and hung up.

I called Angelo from in his plastic chair by the pool and he followed me into the kitchen as we moved away from the patio door.

"Angelo, Spider was murdered this morning in his cell, with poison," I told him.

He stared at me and then shook his head in disbelief, "Poison, that was Spider's favorite way ta kill, that and a slit ta the throat. Feds know anything?"

"Don't know much, Deacon is going to see what he can. Do you have anyone you can call to find out what may have happened?"

Mortuary Murders

"I don't have much pull with the Feds, they don't care much for us. But I have a couple contacts I can call, may help." He pulled his cell phone and excused himself. I let him have his space in the kitchen and went to the patio door to look out at Francis and Penny sitting by the BBQ that I had ready to fire up for the steaks I bought late last night at the all night grocery. I didn't want this to break up our picnic so I resolved to let Deacon handle it.

I waited and then Angelo came back saying his friends would let him know. We both went out and I fired up the adobe monolith that was our BBQ and cooked the steaks while Penny and Francis went into the kitchen to whip up a side dish.

We had finished eating and my cell phone rang again. Penny gave me a dirty look and I shrugged my shoulders and went to answer. It was Deacon.

"What's the word?"

"Special Agent Carlton is not returning my calls. This is really bugging me. I'm going to see if I can get some info on this Fasel Nabib that Spider mentioned. I'm sure I'll run into a brick wall but it's worth looking into."

"Don't step on the Fed's toes, proceed with caution and stealth."

"I will, I'll let you know what I find. How's your party going?" he asked.

"Good, we just had nice juicy steaks and now we are relaxing. They told me they are going back to New York tomorrow morning, I'm going to drive them to the commercial hangers where they have their private jet, then I'll call to see if you need me."

He thanked me and we hung up. Penny was standing behind me and asked, "More murder?"

"Yep, the thug that Angelo delivered to us. Murdered in his cell this morning."

"Doesn't surprise me, they drop dead whenever you're involved," she said with a big smile then went to the kitchen to get some more drinks for everyone; I helped.

Angelo called me aside and asked if I heard anything more from Deacon, I said I hadn't, "Deacon said that he was checking on a possible terrorist named Fasel Nabib, does that name ring any bells?"

"Nope, but I'll get my people on it for ya."

"Anything can help. The man is in town to start an attack on the President when he comes to town next week, that's between you and I. The Feds are supposed to be working on it but with the murder of Spider, I wonder if they are capable of stopping it."

"I'll make some inquiries and let you know."

I thanked him and he went off to make a call. I knew his people were connected around the country and with many unions, so he may come up with something. Anything would help right now.

He came back and said his people would let him know what they find and we went back to sit with the women.

Around 10, we were wearing down so I drove them back to the hotel and then Penny and I took a slow drive up the strip. I always loved to watch the millions of lights flashing and moving. Traffic was light, surprisingly, so we had no problems going along slowly. I turned the limo back towards the house and into the garage. Penny went in to find Willy had dragged out the food again.

Next morning I got ready to go take our friends back to their jet, Penny said to wish them well, she had to go to her studio. I drove over to the Tropicana and pulled into the main entrance. Angelo and Francis were waiting since I called ahead to say I was on my way. The two huge wiseguys were with them, I wondered what they got into while we were doing our thing. We drove out Tropicana and down Russell to the airport and over to the commercial hangers. The big men took the luggage out and into the jet, it was a sleek Gulf Stream and the pilot was standing by.

Angelo took me aside and said, "I got a call this morning, my people say Nabib is a dangerous man, he has loose ties to the Al-Qaeda. He's suppose ta be gathering his army ta cause problems all over the U.S. and they are starting here. There's word of a bomb involved. That's all I got, hope it helps ya."

"It may my friend, so good to see you again. Maybe Penny and I can come out one day to visit your home again."

"Dat would be nice," he said and gave me a bear hug that almost made me lose my breath. He released me and smiled, "Till next time." Then he went to the jet, up the ramp with a wave and went in. The door closed and I stood watching as the jet taxied out and finally getting clearance took off into the wild blue.

**

Chapter 20

Trapper was sitting on the stool watching his lady sleeping quietly in a chair with her head on her brother's bedside. Philip, now Phyllis, was also sleeping off the drugs given during the long surgery. Trapper quietly pulled his cell phone and made a call.

"Hey Jim, how's everything with your case?" he asked.

"Well, there's so much to tell you. Not over the phone though, when you coming back?"

"Hopefully tomorrow, depending on Sam's sister's condition. We will leave her here for a week while she heals and then come back when she's to be released."

"You're using the she designation now."

"Yep, the operation was successful and Philip is now Phyllis. Sam's still a little confused, but happy. I'll give her as much support as I can until she's good with it."

"I'm sure it has to be strange, good that you're there, I'll see you when you get back."

"Yes, my friend you will." He hung up and put his phone back in his pocket.

Sam lifted her head, pushed the hair out of her face and said, "I'm glad you are here too, and I'm starting to be good with it."

"You were listening in on my conversation, not nice."

"I never said I was nice," she said with a big smile. She looked to her new sister sleeping

129

peacefully and said, "I'll give her as much support as I can also."

Trapper got up and went to her, bending down to kiss her gently on the forehead, "We'll both be supportive."

~~*~~

I put my cell phone back in my pocket after talking to Trapper. As soon as I did that, it rang again. I grudgingly pulled it back out and saw it was Deacon.

"Hey, big guy, what's up?"

"I had a strange visit earlier; I got a call from the front desk that there was someone here to see me. I went up front and found a really huge guy with a crew cut and no neck. He hands me a manila envelope and says that it's a present from Angelo. Then he turns and walks out. I was hoping it wasn't a letter bomb but opened it. You need to stop by."

"Wow, I just put Angelo and his mom on their jet. What was in it?"

"Come in and we can go over it." That was all he said and hung up. I hate the mysterious ways he does things sometimes. I pointed my car in the direction of LVMPD and parked upon arrival.

I found Deacon in Lynn's office and sat in front of the desk. "Okay what have you got?"

He smiled and looked to the door just as Lynn walked in. "Hey Lynn, you're back," I said.

"Yep, drove in early this morning. All the time I waited out in LA and the lawyers had me on the stand for all of ten minutes, then cut me loose. Stupid system. Deacon filled me in on the cases you two have been chasing. Now this comes up." She held up the manila envelope and gave Deacon a look, he got out of her chair quickly, and she sat.

"So what did Angelo send you that he couldn't give to me?" I asked.

"This didn't come directly from Angelo, but he got the ball rolling with his contacts here in Vegas. As I told you back when we were chasing the Bridezilla killer, I'm not fond of the mob, but this is good and it will help us," Lynn said.

"You don't like the mob because your father worked for them, that's why you became a cop. So maybe the mob put you on the right course."

She gave me her look and said, "Don't defend your little friends; I would have become a cop anyway. I had a talk with Weber about the contents of this envelope and he agrees that we need to proceed with caution. Now this is what we have here," she said as she pulled out a small stack of papers.

She spread the sheets and I saw pictures of four men who looked to be of Muslim descent. The photos were attached to descriptive info on each man. "This man," pointing to one photo, "is Fasel Nabib, from Afghanistan and he is part of Bin Laden's Jihad. Or so the papers say, we haven't verified anything yet, but it would mean bringing in the FBI and as you know, we don't really want to do that. Deacon told me all about Agent Ross Carlton, and I don't trust him either. Think about it, Carlton had access to

Horace Worley and then Worley turns up dead in a cell in FBI lockup. That sounds fishy to me. Either way, we're going to proceed on this quietly and see where it leads. Deacon filled me in on the attack on the President, and subsequent bomb threat, so that means Las Vegas PD has a stake in protecting our city and our leader."

"So what do the papers tell us?" I asked.

"We have very sketchy info on the location of these men; the papers are basically dossier on each man and their parts in the Jihad. Where the mob got this info, I don't want to know. I'm going to put out Nabib's photo on the LEIN as a suspect in the murder of the funeral director and John Hall. I just hope the FBI doesn't get wind of it."

"I know that Hall was murdered because of his participation in the union negotiations that may have screwed up their plan if the union went on strike, but where does Spenser, the funeral guy fit into it? What key did he hold to their plan of attack?" I asked.

"Well, it's a mystery for now, you and Deacon can follow up on it since you already have started an investigation. I'll start to set up an investigation on our little terrorist friend, Nabib, and see if we can bring him out of the woodwork. I now have a friend in the FBI that taught the training I did out in Langley, I'll see if I can trust him to dig for more info on this." She handed Deacon a couple sheets of the papers, keeping Nabib's sheet, and said, "Follow up on these, and keep your heads low."

We left the building just as Weber was coming into the squad room, missing him by seconds. He probably would have talked our heads off and so it was good that we escaped. Deacon pulled a car out of the motor pool and we sat in it trying to figure out our next move.

"Did you ever wonder who this agent is that Lynn met while in training out in Langley?" I asked.

"She told me all about him, his name is Troy Westlake and he works in terrorist investigations for the bureau. He was Lynn's instructor for counter-terrorism classes."

"Troy? He sounds like a beach bum, must be handsome too."

"Nah, I saw Lynn's photos of her class and he's not that good looking." He went quiet for a beat, then said, "Okay so he is a hunk, but Lynn told me he was married. I trust Lynn."

"Good boy, keep that attitude up and you'll go far."

Deacon gave me a look and drove out from the parking lot. "Where are we going?" I asked.

"This top sheet says that the person in question hangs out at a bar in China town. It may be strange but they may have connections to Chairman Mao."

"Deacon, Chairman Mao has been dead for years."

"Okay, so I don't keep up on world affairs."

"You do know that Stalin is dead also."

"Now you're being cruel, leave me alone."

"Well, your demeanor is certainly rough, didn't Lynn make you happy this morning?"

"No, she got back and we came in to the precinct right away. I was a bit miffed about it. She could have given me a little time. I'm usually good for about ten minutes if we are in a rush."

"Ten? Wow, you are a dynamo. I'm sure she'll make up for it later."

"I hope so, some of the hookers they brought in on a sweep this morning looked mighty good." He glanced sideways to me and then laughed.

We drove over to the section of town where there were a number of Chinese stores and businesses and found the Wing Ho Bar in the middle of the block of buildings. We drove around back and parked, finding a back door to the place and went in. Deacon had already pulled the photos of the men out from the folder and put them in his jacket pocket.

We entered the building finding it dark with many red lights around the perimeter of the room. There were a number of booths that had high partitions, so the customers had somewhat privacy. Deacon smiled and said that there was a bit of prostitution going on here.

"Well, can you get Chinese take-out here?" I joked.

He gave me a grin and said, "I like the peeking goose."

"Just don't let Lynn catch you peeking."

We went up to the bar and a number of women in tight Chinese garb suddenly slid off their stools and headed for the door.

"Do we look like cops?" Deacon asked me.

"You do, I look like someone's grandfather out for a good time."

He leaned on the bar and the woman behind the

counter asked what we wanted.

"Just some info," he said as he pulled the photos from his pocket, "Do you recognize any of these men?"

She gave us a stern look and said in broken English, "I never see them, it would be good for you if you never see them."
**

Chapter 21

Deacon pulled out his badge and showed her, "You sound like you know these gentlemen, tell me about it."

"You crazy, I no get myself killed. Talk to Won Ho, he no care." She pointed to a rather enormous oriental man in his forties sitting at a table by the front door.

"He the boss man?" Deacon asked.

"He just man who bounces people who screw with us. Not man you mess with either."

Deacon pulled a five from his pocket and his card, giving it to the woman. "If you remember anything," he said as we went to Won Ho.

Deacon stood before the huge man and just watched him.

"Watcha want copper?" the man spoke.

"Just some info, a location for a couple bad guys, maybe they came here to indulge in your lovely women."

The man grinned a mouth full of bad teeth and said, "Sit copper, we talk maybe."

Deacon pulled the chair out and sat, I sat on a chair at the next table. Deacon leaned in with the pictures and showed them to Won Ho. The man studied the pictures and grinned again. "Yah, dey come in here plenty time, to tickle the girls. Why you look for them?"

"They plan to do a very bad thing soon and we have to stop them. The bad thing will hurt many people and you don't want to be responsible for hurting many people do you?"

"I don't care for many people, just my people in here. My family."

Well, what these men want to do will hurt your family, big time, if we don't stop them. Tell me what you know."

He sat looking at Deacon through red veined eyes and rubbed his short stubble, thinking. He looked around the room and then turned back to Deacon. "They are part of a group, crazy men, who come here, I throw out couple times but they come back, say sorry and then do the same crap. I throw them out again. I don't want them here, they stink up place. You will make them stop?"

"If you help me, I'll put them out of your way."

"They are staying at cheapy motel on Koval, I know from my brother, taxi driver, he tell me. It's is the Blue Moon motel, all I know. Now you put them out."

Deacon smiled and stood. "I'll do my best to put them away. I'll let you know." We went back out through the rear entrance and to the car.

"Well, we need to go to the Blue Moon and see if our boys are there. Hopefully they're home."

We got ready to drive out as Deacon called on his cell to Warren, explained the situation and told him to gather about six men and meet him at the motel. He hung up and then we drove in silence.

We arrived at the run down motel, and parked by the office. Deacon and I went in, up to the front desk of the motel and an elderly woman stood behind the counter, with a cigarette hanging from her mouth. She looked at the two of us and said, "I don't discriminate, you two want a room to screw, just don't mess the room, got it?"

Deacon laughed and pulled his badge, "We aren't a couple ma'am, are you the manager?"

"I am, what do you want?" she spoke through a smoke abused throat.

"I need to know if these men came here to rent a room?" He pulled the photos and showed her.

"They look the same, but yeah, I think they're here."

"What room are they in?"

"You got a warrant?"

"I'm not entering their room without permission, I'll knock on the door peacefully, now what room are they in?"

She studied Deacon for a moment and then looked to me. "The three of them are in room eight, but you bust it up I'll sue the city, understand."

"Yes, ma'am, we'll try to leave it as we found it." Deacon smiled and we went out as three patrol cars were pulling into the parking lot. Warren stepped out of one car and came to Deacon. "Room eight everyone," he yelled to the men and they all went down to the door. Deacon came up and knocked then stepped aside as he listened for movement.

He heard nothing and tried to see in the window but the curtain was closed. He went to the door again and stood listening, then heard glass breaking and yelled for his men to go around back. He brought his foot up and smashed in the door, then entered with his weapon drawn. There were two men trying to get out through the bathroom window as Deacon came up behind them. He reached up, grabbed the pants of the man just half out of the window and pulled him back in. The man fell into the tub and held his hands up.

Deacon called for the officers to cuff him, read him his rights and take him in. The cops that went around the back had chased the other man and finally pulled him down a few blocks over. They returned with him in cuffs and threw him in the car with the first man.

Deacon looked again to the pictures, then to the men and was satisfied he had the right men.

"We got two now, we need to find the other one along with Nabib. I'm wondering why the FBI didn't find them this easy. Maybe Carlton is in on it."

"It would explain a lot," I said.

Deacon looked at the door he busted in, "That's going to piss off the manager."

Warren came out of the room saying there was nothing in there other than clothes and personal items, nothing pointing to a bomb or death threats on the President. Deacon and I went back to his car and drove out.

We arrived back at the precinct and the two men were put in separate interrogation rooms as we entered the squad room. Weber was standing outside the rooms watching the men.

"Are these the terrorists?" he asked as we came up.

"They match the photos even though their wallets came up with a few pieces of ID, saying they are someone else, so we have them on identity fraud if nothing else. I'm running checks on fingerprints from the new printscanner, but I think they won't be in the system. I'm hoping the Feds don't flag our print search and come busting in. If I see Carlton one more time, I'll shoot the bastard."

Weber actually laughed out loud, I was surprised and then he went off after saying, "Good work".

Deacon looked like he just won the national spelling bee, he was delighted that he got approval from Weber.

"Okay, shall we go find out what our terrorists have to say?" He walked to the first door and entered, I went to observation to watch. The man identified in the dossier from the local mafia said he was Asad Hassam, a soldier for the Afghanistan Liberation Army, a front for bin Laden's people. He sat looking miserable; I thought he wasn't much of a terrorist.

Deacon sat across from the man and just stared.

Mortuary Murders

It was a tactic that Lynn used a lot, to psych the perp out. The man stared back as they just sat there staring at each other. I wondered who would crack first, Deacon or the terrorist.

The man finally turned his head towards the door and coughed. Deacon just waited.

The man finally spoke, "You have no reason to hold me or intrude on my rights."

"Then why were you trying to run from us? We just wanted to talk; it looked suspicious. Like maybe you're trying to hide something."

"I'm hiding nothing, I did no wrong. In my country when the police come to your door you either run or be thrown in prison without a trial."

"Well this isn't your country, so why don't you learn our ways. Maybe you are hiding something that you are plotting?"

The man gave Deacon a wary eye and then said, "I am hiding nothing, I'm a good citizen of the U.S. and I respect the laws."

"A good citizen? Yes, your fake ID's show that you are, but your real ID is something else. We'll find out who you really are shortly. Now tell me about your plans to attack our President?" Deacon threw out his hole card and waited to see what the man would do.

The man did his stare again and showed no emotion, he evidently was trained well to withstand interrogation.

Deacon stood and said, "Okay, play dumb, we'll just wait for your prints to come back and see who you really are." He turned and went out of the room.

He smiled at me and we went to the next room. Deacon tried something different with this man. He was identified as Kahlid Masood and he sat upright in his chair looking defiant. His dossier said he was a lieutenant in the same army as Hassam.

"How you doing Kahlid?" Deacon asked with no expression. Masood just sat motionless. "I'm just coming to you as a courtesy, Hassam was giving us all the details on the assassination attempt on the President and the bomb you guys may use. Not a nice thing to do now is it."

Masood's eyes flickered a bit, I could see it through the trick mirror from the observation room. His defiant smile was turning down slowly and his face took on a less than defiant look. He still stared at Deacon but I could tell he was calculating the information that Deacon had given him. I figured he'd think about Hassam and wonder if the man actually would crack so soon.

"I want a lawyer," was all he said.
**

Chapter 22

"Lawyer? A lawyer? That's something for real citizens of the United States to invoke. You have no rights under our laws; I just may call the Homeland Security people and turn you over to them. Now if you want to talk about your personal involvement in the assassination attempt, maybe I'll keep you away from them. It's your decision. Hassam made his decision, and he's going to coast but we need to backup his statements, you can do that."

Deacon sat back and waited.

Masood went quiet, he was starting to formulate his thoughts. "I want to talk to Hassam."

"No, you can't! Don't screw with us, Masood. We only care about what your mission is and if we don't get verification about what Hassam told us, we will turn you over to the Feds, and they can deal with you. You ever hear about something called waterboarding? Hunh, Masood?"

"I'm not talking," was all he said now.

Deacon pushed the table hard towards Masood, pinning him against the wall. Masood yelped and protested. Deacon stood and gave the table an extra shove and walked out of the room. I came out of observation quickly.

"Damn, this pisses me off. These terrorist come into our country and plot and scheme and kill and we have to be nice to them! I'm all for torture. Beat the crap out of them." Deacon went back into the other room with Hasaam and sat back in front of him. I went into observation again.

"Listen to me scum bag, Masood is ratting you out, he says you're the mastermind behind the plot to assassinate the President and blow up everyone with a bomb. Now what do you have to say about it?"

"I am not the man in charge! I don't have anything to do with organizing the plot. It's Nabib's plot, not mine," he said quickly.

"Well, Masood is talking, but we can't believe

him without you verifying his statements. Maybe we'll believe you and put him away for good."

"Yes, you could put him away, he is not a good man, he is evil. He and Nabib are cousins, they are both evil." He was in a panic now, nearly standing up at his chair as he leaned over the table to Deacon. Deacon pushed him back in his seat.

"Settle down Asad, just go slowly and tell me what you know."

Asad sat back and was collecting his thoughts, "I came into America as a tourist, we got false identifications from Nabib's contacts here. From our soldiers who have been in the country for months. We were getting the mission set up with them and then we would take over. They would go to another United States city to set up an attack there with the bombs we bought from the Russians."

Russians? I didn't think they would still be in the arms business, with all their troubles they were having. But I guess if they needed money, so they could sell off a few small devices to these terrorists.

"What kind of bombs, Asad?" Deacon asked.

"You call them dirty bombs, they spread radiation all around, make everything unusable for years. Kill off many people, show them we mean business about our plight."

"What plight, Asad?"

"Our Jihad, our religious right to destroy all the infidels who mock our religion, it is part of what we believe. Death to non-believers," he said with a scary conviction.

"Well, Asad, don't you know this country allows

people to believe whatever they want, including Muslims. That's what makes our country great and better than your restrictive beliefs." Deacon stood and waved to the uniform standing outside the room and told him to put Asad in a holding cell.

"You are going to kill me now, put me in your prison cell and then they find me dead, that's the way you do things," he yelled at Deacon.

Deacon looked to the cop and said, "See that he dies quickly." They both laughed and the cop took Asad out.

Deacon turned to the glass and pointed out to the squad room. I left observation and over to him. "What's the plan now? We know what they are planning, but where are they setting up shop to get the mission in gear?" I said.

Deacon gave me a finger follow motion and went back to Masood's room. I went into observation again; I should get frequent flyer mileage on my trips to these rooms.

Deacon went in and sat again. He related everything Asad told him as Masood sat listening emotionless.

"I don't really need you to verify his statements, but I don't trust your friend, he is probably lying about you being the head man in this attack. Your cousin Nabib is still on the loose, but we will find him."

I saw a flicker in Masood's eye when Deacon mentioned that Nabib was his cousin. Only Asad could have told Deacon that.

"Exactly what has that idiot Hassam told you?" he asked.

"Well, it's a matter of police record now, as you have been told, we record all conversations in these rooms. But you won't have access to Hassam's testimony; you just worry about your own neck."

Deacon was doing his best to play one man against the other. It's something that works well when you can keep the perps separated in these rooms where they have no access to the other person. Plus, the police can tell tall tales, well actually tell subtle lies, and get away with it.

"My cousin Fasel will continue our mission with or without us, he is resourceful and can replace us with the many of our soldiers here in your sinful city."

"That's Sin City, Kahlid, and you wouldn't understand the meaning of that. You are repressed and still in the fourth century where they carry on religious wars that prove nothing but killing good people. You are scum Masood, do you know what scum is? It's the crap under your shoes when you walk through a cow pasture. That's what you are." Deacon got up again and left the room.

Deacon came into observation and sat with me. "Think I was a little too harsh with him?"

"I think you should have beaten the crap out of him, but then Weber would have you on the carpet. Either way you did good," I said.

He smiled at me and said, "Thanks."

Mortuary Murders

Lynn came busting into the room and was all worked up, "We found Nabib! I got the warrant, shall we go pick him up?"

We both jumped from our seats and followed Lynn to the back of the building, after Deacon told a cop to put Masood in a cell. Lynn turned to us before we went out of the building and said, "We ran checks watching for credit cards that Nabib may have tried to use. He was such a vain person that he used his own name. He's also indulging in the trappings of the sinfulness of this city, he's staying at the Bellagio Hotel and is ordering all kinds of room service. Some devotion to Allah, he's enjoying our wicked ways."

We all went to cars waiting in the motor pool and drove out to the Bellagio Hotel. All five cars pulled up to the valet parking and the parking attendants didn't know what to do. Lynn yelled for them to leave the cars alone and we all streamed into the lobby. Lynn went to the counter, flashed her badge and said to tell her the room number of Fasel Nabib. The girl behind the counter look flustered and called the supervisor over and Lynn went through it again showing the warrant. The supervisor told the clerk to get us the room number and she did.

We arrived on the tenth floor and found the room. Lynn had everyone stand to the sides and stood in front of the peephole so just her face was seen. She knocked on the door and waited, there came a call through the door asking who it was and Lynn responded saying room service. There was a pause and then we heard the door unlock and slowly open. Lynn shoved the door, pushing the person back and everyone rushed in with weapons drawn.

There was one man in the large, expensive room. He looked in a panic at the sight of all the police now sweeping the room for others, but finding none. Lynn went to the man and with the photos Deacon gave her, identified the man as Nouri bin Thabot.

"Where's Nabib?!" Lynn demanded of the man.

"He's not here," was all he said.

"Yeah, buckwad, I can see that. Where is he was what I asked."

"I don't know, he left an hour ago and didn't say where he was going."

Lynn turned to a uniform and said to take him in and watch him closely. Then she told everyone to search for anything pointing to their plans. We went through the contents of the room and found a number of papers showing pictures of a weapon that they must have. According to the description, it was a device of great power that could decimate a city about half the size of Las Vegas. Lynn called over one of the forensic people and showed him the paper.

He smiled and said, "The Russian's are promoting this as a weapon of mass destruction, it's not. This bomb combines radioactive materials with conventional explosives that would contaminate a large area around where the bomb is detonated which is why it's called a "dirty bomb" and it's also referred to as an RDD, radiological dispersal device. Tests on such a bomb have shown it to be more dangerous from the explosion than the radioactive materials. The radioactivity would cause illness, but not death as the paper states. Mostly this bomb is more psychological than physical, in that it causes mass panic and fear than actual harm. Don't get me wrong, it will kill but not on the scale that they are promoting."

"So in order to really make people feel unsafe, the terrorist would have to let people know they have the bomb and will use it."

"Right, the bomb in actuality would cause contamination of thousands of people and property that would take considerable time and cost to fix so it would be more of an economic burden on the city. In effect, shutting the city down, which would ruin Vegas."

**

Chapter 23

"Sounds like a personal problem," Deacon said. "Maybe Nabib lost his shirt gambling and is going to ruin us now."

One CSI came up with a plastic bag containing a letter. Lynn read the letter then gave it to Deacon, I read over his shoulder. Well, around his arm since he's about a head taller than I was. It was a statement, it said, "People of the United States, I am giving you a warning, on the 22nd of this month, my people, the Afghanistani Liberation Army will cause great pain to your government, and then a week later we will detonate what is called a dirty bomb in three major cities, Las Vegas, Hollywood and Washington. One each day after the first. Radiation and destruction will be spread everywhere in these cities. You have until midnight of the 29th to surrender all prisoners taken from Afghanistan, removing your troops from our country and provide us with ten billion dollars in gold. To not do so will result in thousands of dead and cities spoiled. Our first attack will show we are serious. Death to non-believers of Allah." It was signed by Nabib.

"Hollywood? I guess Nabib wanted to hit us where it hurts, our entertainment and our valued personalities. I can see Washington, but Hollywood?" Deacon said.

"Celebrities are more popular than politicians, target the right people and we might cave in," I said.

Another CSI came up and said to Lynn, "Lieutenant, I found some invoices that are dated two days before yesterday and some delivery statements. It seems there was only one bomb purchased, and it was delivered to a Las Vegas warehouse over off Industrial Drive. Here's the statement," he finished and handed the paper to Lynn.

"Well, this makes Nabib a con man. He doesn't have the power to carry out his demands, but he has the one bomb so he can scare us into believing he'll do the rest. We have get to the warehouse where they delivered the bomb. Deacon, call for SWAT and the bomb squad to meet us at this address." She handed him the paper and Deacon went out to the hallway to call.

"I'm a little amazed that the Russian's would give

out invoices for their bombs, it sort of proves they are backing these extremists," I said looking at the invoice. "Although it doesn't exactly say 'made in Russia', just that it was shipped from Russia to here as electronic equipment, delivered through of all things, FedEx. I wonder how many other explosive devices are sent through them?"

I was looking at the paper with the description of the bomb, it was about the diameter of a fire hydrant and about three feet tall. To hide this thing would be no problem at all; it could be put just about anywhere.

"Look at it later, we need to get to the warehouse before they can move the thing," Lynn said as she headed towards the door.

I handed the paper back to the CSI and followed her. Deacon was just finishing his call to the precinct and said we were good to go. We all went back down as five uniforms stood guard in the hotel room, mostly waiting to see if Nabib came back.

We drove out Vegas Boulevard and turned onto Tropicana, then down Industrial Drive. We passed my office plaza on the way; I wondered how it was going there. We arrived at the series of warehouses all in a row and up to the address from the delivery sheet. SWAT and a group of black and whites were just streaming down the road behind us.

We all piled out and Lynn had SWAT up front, then her people followed by the bomb squad. She had warned them this was a dirty bomb and the squad leader called to break out radiation equipment to his men. It was a small warehouse, used by small businesses to store their equipment and supplies, but big enough for the operation to gather and plot.

Lynn had already called for an emergency warrant from Weber, based on the delivery papers and we had a go to enter the building. SWAT tried the door, it was locked so they took the ram to it and everyone scrambled into the building. There was no lobby or offices; it was more of a large storage building. In the center of the room were tables and a packing crate, opened. Next to the packing crate was one of those large office photocopiers, its back was open and it had no internal parts, just a hollow shell.

"Well, this is how they shipped the bomb in, faked it as a copier," Deacon said. We looked around as the Bomb Squad had their men checking for radiation.

One man offered, "The copier is lincd with lead sheeting, to hide any radiation, but there is a small amount of residual radiation in the container."

The room was clean, no bomb, no people. The table had diagrams of the route that the President would take on his trip to Vegas and to the County Building where he was to meet with the Mayor and City Council. "I wonder how they got this route plan, it's not public knowledge. I'm wondering if they have a person inside," Lynn said as she studied the papers.

Deacon commented, "Probably Agent Carlton."

Lynn looked to him and nodded. I was just off the side watching everything and wondering where they would have the bomb if it wasn't here. Why would they even take it out if they felt the building was safe for now? They didn't have time to move out if they found out we had invaded the hotel, could they? They left the papers behind, if they had moved things out quickly, dumb move since it gave the plan away. I figured they had removed the bomb before they even knew we attacked the hotel and it was now somewhere else in the city.

Lynn came to me and asked, "Do you think any of your Area 51 buddies could have a stealth plane that can scan the city for radiation? Maybe we could locate it that way."

I thought on it and said, "I'm sure the government has something like that, they have ways of spying on us, and so it's possible. I still have the personal phone number of Major Rickson, the head of Intelligence; he may be able to help. I'll call him." I went off the side, pulled my cell phone, ran through the internal phone book and found the number. He came on after three rings.

"Why are you calling me, Richards, got another dead body?" he said before I even spoke, must have me on his caller ID.

"Major, we have a big problem here in Vegas that you may be able to help with and it also could have a big effect on your base." I explained the situation to him and he was silent the whole time. I finished and he was still silent, I thought he had hung up on me. "Are you still there?"

"I am, I'm thinking. Is the Office of Homeland Security in on this?"

"We just got all this information, so we haven't had time to bring anyone else in on it. I called you first about the radiation seeking equipment you may have," I said.

"We do have the capabilities to do so. But it's a hit and miss thing, especially if the bomb is shielded in anyway. I'll see what I can do by talking to the base commander, he doesn't like his equipment going out without his approval. Damn politics. I'll call you back shortly."

I smiled from hearing his voice again. I hung up and went back to Lynn and Deacon telling them what had transpired. Lynn said, "I don't want to do it, but we may need to bring in the big guns, who shall I call first, Homeland Security or the Feds?"

Deacon said, "Homeland Security, just to screw over Carlton." He laughed to himself as Lynn pulled her phone. She called Weber, explained the situation and asked his advice. Smart, let him take the heat.

She hung up after listening, "He's going to make a few calls and get back to us." She looked relieved.

We wandered the building looking for anything that may help, but it was a sparse area, and not many places to hide things. We stood as an overhead door opened on the other side of the building from where we came in, and all the SWAT people went on point. A man was walking back to the truck that was sitting just outside the opening; he was oblivious to our presence and got into the truck to drive it in.

He was sitting in the cab of the truck as he went forward when he looked into the building and saw us. I could see the panic on his face as he tried to go in reverse but over steered it into the side of the doorway and jammed it. The SWAT had him surrounded now and he held his hands up, gibbering something in what sounded like Arabic. They pulled him from the cab and had him on the ground as they checked him for weapons.

Lynn, Deacon and the Bomb Squad went to the back of the truck and opened it, finding it empty. The Captain of the Bomb Squad had his men scan for radiation and found trace amounts.

"They took the bomb elsewhere and dropped it off. It must be in place for the attack now." She went back to the table with the plans and looked closer for a point on the map showing a possible place for the bomb, but found nothing.

"We got a mystery," she said, then smiled, "Let's beat the crap out of the truck driver, and get the info from him."

*

Chapter 24

SWAT had the man seated in a chair by the table and looking totally frightened. Lynn came up to him, taking her weapon out of it's holster and held it in front of her. I knew she wouldn't shoot him but he didn't know that. From his country, the soldiers liked to shoot their people as they interrogate them.

"Okay monkey guts; talk to me, where's the bomb?"

The man looked puzzled, and spoke something in Arabic. "Crap, doesn't he speak English?" Lynn moaned.

One of the Bomb Squad men spoke up and said, "He says he doesn't understand you."

Lynn looked to the officer and said, "You can speak his lingo, get over here and help."

He looked to his Captain and the Captain nodded to him, he came over next to Lynn and waited for instructions.

"Tell him we will be very harsh on him if he doesn't cooperate." The cop gave him the word. His eyes went big and he gibbered something.

"He says he's just the delivery guy, he has nothing to do with the plot."

"Ask him where he delivered the package, don't call it a bomb. See what he says," Lynn said.

Again, the officer translated and the man started to babble a mile a minute. The cop turned to Lynn when the man finished, "He's going nuts, something about death and cars, I'm sorry but his dialect is now a little different than I understand. He's slipping into slang, but I only understand the higher form of his language, not the gutter talk. But he did mention the bomb and he was afraid he would set it off. He says they put it in a box and then into a car."

"Going mobile with it?" Deacon said. "They could take it anywhere to avoid detection."

"Ask him if he knows where Nabib is?"

He translated and the man spoke only a couple words.

Lynn spoke first, "Don't tell me, he doesn't know."

The cop smiled and said, "You got it."

Lynn turned to her uniforms and said to take him in and get a translator in the precinct to make it easier for them. She thanked the SWAT officer for his help and he went off with his men as the SWAT Captain called them to all recon out in the parking lot. That left us and a couple of Lynn's uniforms in the building now.

"We keep getting close only to be pulled back. But we have all their hideouts secure now, Nabib is going to be pissed when he can't get room service." Lynn laughed through the tension that was building up in her.

"We have three days before the President arrives at McCarran Airport. Maybe you should let the Secret Service know what you have now," I said.

Lynn stood thinking and then agreed. "I think we are taking on more than we can chew. This could be disastrous and we don't have the resources to carry out this task. I can call my FBI friend and get the ball rolling, but I haven't heard from Weber, so we should go back to the station and see what he has first."

Lynn instructed a couple of the officers to hang around and secure the place, just in case Nabib showed here. We went back to Lynn's unmarked car and headed back to the precinct.

I got out of the car and said, "If anything happens, let me know, I'm going to my office to see what's going on there. I'll talk later if the Major calls about the plane."

Lynn thanked me and I went to my car in the parking lot, drove over to my building and parked in the back. I came in through the back door and yelled out loud, "I'm here!" I was startled by a scream, looked over to the storeroom next to the back entrance and saw Lacey in the room.

"Damn, you just keep scaring me no matter where I am in the building. Stop yelling!" She huffed up towards the front with file folders in her arms. I laughed quietly so not to make her mad and followed.

I peeked into Buck's office and he was sitting back in his chair on the phone. I waved, he waved back and I went up front to find Penny sitting on a couch with Willy watching a movie on the TV. She saw me and gave me a wave as I came to her.

"How long have you been here?" I asked.

"About two hours, this movie is almost over, sit and watch it with me."

I sat needing the rest and put my head back on the couch, then I must have drifted off because Penny was shaking me and calling in my ear, "Wake up." I looked around with groggy eyes and then focused on Penny who was giving me a big smile. "Was the movie good," I asked.

"It was alright, I didn't like the ending, they always finish these movies so you are confused. How was your day?"

"Oh, we chased terrorists and they have a nuclear device that they are going to set off next week, but we can't find the bomb."

She studied my face for a moment then said, "You love telling stories don't you. Now what did you really do?"

"Just what I said, geez, I'm telling the truth."

"Okay, we're moving back to Michigan, last month it was a terrorist with a virus, and now terrorists with nuclear weapons in Vegas, it's getting too dangerous here."

"That's what I said, but we're getting close to stopping them, we caught most of the men involved, just need the leader of the gang and we may have it solved. Although, we still need to find the bomb."

Willy crawled over to me and plopped down on my lap, I scratched his ears and then Penny kissed my cheek. "What was that for?" I asked.

"Just for being you, and for protecting our city from bad guys." She kissed me again, this time on the lips.

"You need to really thank me later at home," I said with a smile.

"We'll see." She got up, went to the counter and asked Lacey if she was interested in going shopping.

I tilted my head back from the couch and said, "Hey, we have a business to run here, besides it's almost 4 PM, we will be closing down in an hour."

"I need something to wear for bedtime, if you must know; something frilly, black and silky. Or I could forget it."

"No, no. Go and I'll see you at home," I said and she kissed me again. Lacey gathered her purse and came around the counter; they went out front to Penny's car and drove off as I watched. I looked to Willy and said, "I guess it's just you and me now."

Buck came out of from the hallway and plopped down on the other couch. "So Jimmy how's life?"

"Well, still trying to save Vegas from mass destruction, otherwise good."

"I'm starting a new hiring program; I'm getting rid of a few guards who are not performing well."

"Just be sure you fire them with just cause or they'll be suing"

"I had the clause in their contracts that said they would be let go with three warnings of any infraction of my rules of conduct. I have four now who are just one infraction from being sacked." He smiled and stretched out on the couch.

"Don't fall asleep there, if a client comes in, they will wonder if we allow homeless to crash here," I joked.

"I may be grubby, but I'm not homeless," he mumbled.

"Speaking of homeless, how is Maria, I don't see her too much anymore."

"She's always busy with her show at the Tropicana. I go in to watch it ever so often; they try new things so she rehearses quite a bit. Although she has mentioned about retiring, all that dancing and bouncing her boobs around the stage every night is wearing on her. She said she had an offer to work in one of the casinos as a hostess. She may take it, fewer hours so we can spend more time together."

"That sounds good; you need a steady home life, so you aren't here all the time, sleeping on the couch."

Buck didn't say anything, then I heard him start snoring. Oh, well.

I picked up Willy and stood, going to my private

159

office and sat at the computer. I checked my emails, got one from my publisher asking if I had my latest book finished yet. I shot off a reply saying that I was on a case that would be a spectacular plot for the next book and sent it. I read other emails and then closed the computer down. I looked to Willy who was now resting on the chair next to me and said, "Shall we go home and see what mommy has to wear for me tonight, something sexy I hope." I stood picking up the pup and went back to see if Buck was awake now, he was gone. I went to his office and he was on the phone again. He paused and I said I was leaving, he said good night and I took the dog and myself to my car. We drove out thinking about the day and wondering if we would find the bomb, although Nabib had said he wouldn't detonate it until a week from the arrival of the President. We still had time.

I arrived home and parked the car in the garage, saw that Penny's car was parked and went in to the kitchen. I heard penny call from the living room and went in to find her wearing one of those full pajamas that have the feet, she was covered from neck to toe in flannel. I was a bit shaken by the outfit.

She smiled and slowly zipped down the front of the thing slowly revealing a hint of black lace, she pulled the opening wider and I could see the sexy teddy better now.

"That was mean, you are going to be spanked for that," I said as she ran towards the bedroom, I followed.

**

Chapter 25

The next morning I arrived at the office and went in the front door this time figuring I wouldn't scare Lacey. She was not at her desk, but the doorbell tinkled and she must have heard that. I went down the hallway as she was coming out of the restroom and saw me in the hall, screamed and then she realized it was me.

"Okay, I'll call on my cell phone as soon as I get into the parking lot so I don't give you a heart attack!" I said quickly before she started on me.

She just gave me a stare, walked around me and went to her desk; I went to my office. I was sitting at my desk when Trapper walked in startling me. This was going to be a day of frightening people I guess.

"Hey Will, when did you get back?" I asked.

"Very late last night. We drove all the way through from Denver because Sam had to get back to her business. Ten hours driving all seven hundred fifty miles. We took turns," he replied.

"Which business did she need to get back to, the hair salon or the bookie back room?" I smiled.

"Both. Did you finish up the missing body case?"

"Well, there's been a new twist to it." I explained everything from when I talked to him last. He just sat taking it all in, shaking his head every so often. "Now we have to find Nabib and the bomb."

"That would be a good name for a band, 'Nabib and Da Bomb', okay maybe not," he said with a wink.

"Well I'm waiting to hear from Lynn or Deacon

161

before I make any plans. I want to hear about your trip out in Denver, tell me later when we can relax longer."

"Shall do. Now do you have a hot case for me to work?"

"Sorry but it's been slow. You can help on the terrorist plot; we need all the people we can get to work it."

"I'll do my best, now what say we amble over to Metro and see what we can stir up."

I thought for a moment and said, "Why not, we'll just end up there anyway. I'll let Lacey know and we can head out. Let's take separate cars just in case." He agreed and I went out to the front whistling like a bird and popped out, this time Lacey was watching me arrive and smiled. I told her where Trapper and I were going and to call if anything bad turns up. I peeked into Buck's office but he wasn't there, so I met Trapper by my office and said I was out front.

"Why are you parking out there?" he asked.

"Long story, I'll tell you later." I went to get my car, drove over to Metro and parked. Trapper drove in after me and pulled up next to my car. We went in through the back door toward Lynn's office. There was a lot of commotion in the squad room, more people than usual. I saw a number of black suits and figured they called in the Feds.

Deacon saw Trapper and me and came over. "Weber called Homeland Security and the Feds, and now everyone is stumbling over each other for jurisdiction."

"Is Agent Carlton around?" I asked.

"Nope, he hasn't shown his face yet. I'm waiting for him to appear any moment; I want to needle him about letting Spider get murdered."

Trapper asked, "Feds are killing spiders now?"

"No, Spider is, or was, a hit man from Jersey, I thought I explained that to you."

"I guess I wasn't listening," he smiled.

"So we are now the official center for terrorist bombing activities in Las Vegas. Everyone is stumbling over each other; it's like watching a Keystone Cops comedy," Deacon said.

Lynn came over and told us, "We need to get out of here, this is insane. Hi Will, good to see you are alive and well."

"Barely, I drove in from Denver last night and I'm a bit slow this morning. Anything I can do to help, I'm here."

"Thanks, We've got a lead that I haven't shared with the Feds yet, I think we need to get out of here, no one will notice we're gone."

We went out the back door and stood in the parking lot. Lynn told Deacon to tell us what he knew. "I got a call from the guy who's the bouncer in the Wing Ho bar," he looked to me, "you remember him. Well, he got my card from the woman bartender and called, he said he had some info on Nabib. I never mentioned Nabib to him just the other men in the group, so I'm wondering how he knew. But it's something to look into."

"Shall we go check it out?" Lynn said to us. Lynn and Deacon went to their unmarked car and I took Trapper in mine since I knew the way there.

We arrived and parked in back again. Lynn said, "Trapper and I can go in first and sit at the bar and watch. Deacon and Jim will go in and talk to this guy. We'll watch your backs."

Trapper and Lynn went in as Deacon and I waited a good five minutes then entered the back door. The place still looked the same, Trapper and Lynn were seated at the bar looking like a couple of tourist out for a drink. Won Ho was still at the table by the front entrance. He saw us and gave his big toothy grin, motioning us to come over.

We went and sat back in the seat we were in the other day.

"You guys take out the bad ones?" he asked.

"The men in the pictures we showed you are all under arrest and probably will go to federal prison, so they are gone," Deacon said.

"That be good."

"How did you know about Nabib? I never mentioned him when we talked," Deacon asked.

"Him come in here early this morning looking for his men. He says to me to let him know if they come around. I got his number."

Deacon perked up on that and asked where it was.

Won Ho reached to his shirt pocket, then took out a slip of paper and then looked to the back of the room. I was sitting there wondering why Nabib would give this man his number, when I turned my head and saw two men standing in the back corner of the room, opposite from Trapper and Lynn. They had automatic weapons.

I yelled "Guns," and dove towards Deacon knocking him off his chair as the men started firing. Lynn and Trapper pulled their weapons and spun around firing back at the men. They didn't know that Lynn and Trapper were with us, or cops, so they were taken by surprise. Both men were hit and dropped to the floor. I came up with my Glock drawn and pointed it at Won Ho's face, close.

"Not smart! Talk now, what do you know or you are a dead man, caught in the crossfire!"

Deacon came off the floor with his weapon drawn and held it in Won Ho's ear. "He's right, a bullet to your fat head from all the gunfire in the room, so sorry, you were in the way. Talk now!"

Won Ho sat quietly weighing his options, he spoke, "I was told by this Nabib to do away with anyone who came to ask about his operation. I follow orders or he kills me."

"Not much of a choice. Murder or be murdered. Now do you know where Nabib is hiding out? Again think carefully, I can pull this trigger and get away with it," Deacon said.

He said, "You can pull the trigger, but I would still have to say I don't know. He knows me, I not know him." He went silent and closed his eyes. Deacon and I put our guns away and looked back as Lynn and Trapper were checking the bodies of the men they shot.

"Are these your men or Nabib's?" Deacon asked.

He spoke without opening his eyes, "They are from a local Tong gang, but they work through Nabib."

165

"Tong, I thought that was only in movies," I said to Deacon.

"There are a couple Tong gangs in Vegas, them and a Triad gang, small and not much muscle. But they are a pain in the ass at times. Mostly keep to themselves and fight among each other. If Nabib is gathering steam through the Tongs, this can't be good."

Lynn came over after she called for back-up and the ME. "Did I hear mention of the Tongs?"

"Yep, Nabib is recruiting them evidently. Won Ho here is just an innocent bystander in this assassination attempt on us. Aren't you Ho?"

Won Ho opened his eyes and nodded carefully.

Deacon explained what Won Ho had told him, then said, "I think we should put Mr. Ho in protective custody, he may be helpful in finding Nabib. A nice cell for the night may bring out some memories of Nabib's activities."

Lynn agreed and we waited for the troops to arrive. After about ten minutes, Warren came in the building followed by four officers and the assistant ME. Lynn instructed Warren to have Won Ho taken in to sit overnight in holding, until she could figure what to do with him. Warren had all four of the officers take charge of Won Ho and the big man didn't fight, he went quietly, until they got out the back door when a rifle shot put his life to an end.

**

Chapter 26

We all ran to the back door and Lynn carefully looked out. The officers outside were all scattered and were covered behind their patrol cars. Won Ho was flat out on his back, blood leaking from his chest. There was no more gunfire, Lynn and Deacon ran to different cars and carefully looked around. There were way too many places for a hitman to set up a spot to shoot his intended victim.

"How the hell did they know we were going to bring out Won Ho? This reminds me of Reslo's hit." Deacon yelled. I ran over to the car and crouched next to him.

"They probably had the shooter in place in case the hit inside went bad, which it did, for the bad guys," I said.

Lynn called for reinforcements and kept watching for the hitman. About ten minutes later SWAT came roaring up and everyone poured out of the step van, ready to fight. The SWAT Captain told his men to spread out and search the area.

Lynn slowly stood and came over to Deacon and me. We stood also and were watching around, but saw nothing.

One of the officers came running out of the bar and called to Lynn. "Lieutenant, one of the shooters is still alive."

We went back into the building and found the assistant ME was doing his best to give the man aid.

He had called for an EMS and the man was babbling. Lynn leaned down to him and asked where Nabib was?

The man opened his eyes and evidently couldn't focus. "Nabib, is that you?"

Deacon leaned down also and said, "Yes, it is I, tell me where you are taking me back to the hideout?"

The man was rolling his head around, "Can I drive? I'll take you Nabib."

"Where are you taking me?"

"Our building."

"Where is the building, tell me now?"

"You wouldn't know, Nabib. It is well hidden from the police. It is the back building, behind the death house. It is a good hiding place."

"What the hell is he talking about?" Lynn said.

I thought on it and wondered. "I'm thinking it may have something to do with the funeral home. Spenser was murdered by this group, so maybe they are hiding out in some building by the funeral home or in the funeral home. Hannigan said he was doing the embalming for Spenser to save him the cost of doing it himself. Maybe the unused mortuary in the funeral home is where they are hiding."

"Well it's as good as anything I can come up with," Lynn said. "Shall we go?" She turned to an officer and said to follow him into the hospital and watch him carefully.

We all went back out and Lynn told Warren to take charge as we went to our cars. Back in my Crown Vic, Trapper was laughing, "What's so funny?" I asked.

"I come back from Denver to be shot at and now we're going to a funeral home. I've said before, you have the death eye, Jim."

"Don't start that again, I don't have any such death eye, you made that up. You, Earl and Harold out in Tahiti."

"Okay, believe what you will, you got it." He sat in the passenger seat chuckling.

"You're an idiot, Will," I said and went silent the rest of the drive to the funeral home.

I looked in my rear view mirror and saw a number of patrol cars following, Lynn must have called for reinforcements. We arrived on the street where the home was and pulled into the back parking lot. The SWAT van rolled in moments later and The Captain got out and up to Lynn.

"What have you got, Lieutenant?" he asked.

"Don't know, just a hunch. Have your men search all these out buildings for our terrorists," she said.

Lynn motioned to Deacon, Trapper and me to follow. We went up to the main building and the doors were locked. Lynn banged on the door continually, until the woman who we met when we here for Spenser's murder, Miss Hawthorn, came out. She got to the door and unlocked it; she was a bit unnerved seeing all the cops around the area.

"What's going on?" she asked.

"We need to search your building, it's possible that you have a bomb," Lynn said simply. Hawthorn looked even more shocked and opened the door wide and said to come in.

Before we went into the funeral home, we heard a loud yelling and turned to see the SWAT team running towards a very large garage. We ran there and into the open bay door, there were two hearses parked in the building and then we found out why the men were yelling. A body.

Lynn went to the man's body lying on the floor and turned him. He was shot in the head, clean between the eyes. "We have a hitman murdering people. Get Hawthorn in here, now."

Deacon went out, brought the woman in and when she saw the man, she cried out, "Harry!"

"You know this man?" Lynn asked.

"He's our driver for funerals. He drives the hearses." She looked around the room, "One of the hearses is not here, and there was no schedule to take one out. We've been robbed!"

Lynn was going to make a call to put out a BOLO on the hearse but stopped. Deacon said, "What's wrong?"

"If we put out a call to stop hearses, we'll have lawsuits up the ass from distraught families watching us pull over their dearly departed. We have to proceed with caution on this. Get a description and a plate number if possible from the Hawthorne woman and then place the call." Deacon went over to the woman and they went out, probably to get the information.

Lynn looked to me, "This is getting deep doo-doo. We still aren't any closer."

"I remember the Arabic truck delivery guy saying they delivered the bomb and put it in a box and a death car. The bomb may be in a coffin and in the hearse. It's probably hidden for now and waiting for the day to detonate," I said.

"I have to agree, Nabib needs to have the bomb mobile and this would be good, if we hadn't discovered the stolen hearse. Okay, we know what to look for, and where the bomb is being stored. Now to find another damn hiding place where they have the hearse."

"I'm wondering also, this guy shooting our informants with a high powered rifle from who knows where; maybe he's the shooter who will assassinate the President the day after tomorrow. Does he work for Nabib, or a shooter from out of town? I'll call Angelo to see if he knows any really good riflemen who do hits."

Lynn said, "Sounds good to me, let me know what he says. I'm not fond of depending on the mob and I'm not going to owe them, you'll do that." She smiled at me and I went out of the building to call.

"Angelo, it's Jim again. Sorry to bother you but I need some info. Are you free to talk?" He said he was. "I need to know if you can find names of hitmen who are proficient at rifle fire from a long distance. Preferably one who is now in Vegas." I paused while he thought and then said he'd get back to me. I thanked him and disconnected.

I went back to Lynn and told her Angelo would get back to me and we stood not knowing what to do next. Deacon came back in and said, "I called the description and plate ID in and they will be looking out for it. Now what?"

"I feel like just going back to LA and sitting in my nice hotel suite and ordering room service. I came back to death and destruction instead."

As we stood there, FBI Agent Carlton walked in. "Conducting your own investigation now?" he said.

Deacon was shocked to see the man and I held his arm as I saw him tense up. He relaxed a bit then said, "Lynn, this Special Agent Carlton, FBI and the man who let our hitman get killed."

"Hey asshole, I had nothing to do with that. I wasn't even near the building when he was killed. So back off!" Carlton yelled back.

Lynn stepped between the two men as they started to get closer and said, "Okay. Chill, both of you. What do you want Carlton?"

"That's Agent Carlton, I heard your call for back-up and followed the lead here. You evidently have Nabib on the run now. I'm authorized to tell you to back off, as the FBI and the Secret Service is taking over."

"What about Homeland Security?" Lynn asked.

"They are taking the base operations, we are taking the field. Now I want all your intel on Nabib and anything you may have deduced."

"Like hell, Carlton, get your own intel," Deacon spoke loudly. Lynn looked back to Deacon and he quieted down. He looked pissed and walked away. I stood back watching.

"Okay, Agent Carlton, we are always one step behind Nabib. He evidently was hiding out here but he's in the wind, we don't know where."

"I hope you aren't keeping information back from us. That could be real bad for your career."

"Don't threaten me Carlton, you're out of your league here in Vegas. Now go chase little bunnies or get people killed, I don't like you, for the record." She stared down Carlton; he turned and walked away.

Lynn looked to me and said, "I really don't like that man."

**

Chapter 27

We saw more black suits flowing into the funeral home parking now. Lynn looked to Deacon, Trapper and me and said, "Let's get out of here; this place is starting to smell."

Lynn told the SWAT Captain to let the Feds play and his team could go back to base. The Captain called his men and they all boarded the step van.

We went to our cars and as we got there, Lynn said that we should go eat lunch. I liked that idea and we agreed to Carl's Jr. for burgers and fries. We drove out, met at the fast food restaurant on Maryland and went in. We ordered our food and sat at a table by the window.

We didn't talk much, everyone was still a little miffed about the Feds taking over. "Maybe it's for the better; let them take the heat and responsibility," Lynn said.

Mortuary Murders

I said, "You're not going to let it go are you? You're going to continue to investigate."

"Bet your sweet bippy I am. We can still investigate the murder of the funeral director. There was a plot there to kill him, and we are going to follow the trail. Aren't we?" She looked to us and we all nodded. "We'll just wait for the Feds to go back to their cave and we'll check out the funeral parlor again, as a matter of our investigation."

We ate feeling our spirits were a little lighter, then my cell phone rang. I excused myself and answered; it was Angelo.

"Hey Angelo, did out find out anything?"

"Mr. R. you got a real pro shooter out there. His name is Stephen DeMolay, he's an ex-combat mercenary for hire and a dead on shot. Word has it he's in Vegas, the only one we can track down, but my best guess for your shooter. He is reportedly staying at the Monte Carlo Hotel. My hotel union contacts says he's in room 204. Hope that helps."

"Angelo, give yourself a kiss on me and much thanks. Say hi to everyone for me." He said he would and we finished.

I told Lynn what he said and she thought on it. "He's not going anywhere for now, he probably thinks he's safe in his suite. I want to finish my burger and then we'll slowly go there, so not to attract attention from the Feds and see what we have."

We finished our meal and stood out in the parking lot while Lynn called Warren asking where he was. He said, "I'm back at the precinct and it's a mad house of authority and testosterone all trying to save the world. Whatcha got?"

"Okay, listen, I want a small team of the best men, armed and ready, take them to the Monte Carlo, room 204. We'll be near there so watch for us. Don't let on to anyone, keep it on the QT. I don't want to be stumbling over Feds."

"Got it, Lieutenant, see you there." He hung up, Lynn said to us, "We don't even know if he's there, he could be out entertaining himself. If we can get in his room maybe we can surprise him." She finished and we went to our cars.

The Monte Carlo came up quickly as we weren't very far away. We pulled into the parking structure and found Warren and his men already there. "You move fast Greg," she said with a grin.

"These guys were still suited up from the funeral parlor, so I just gathered them and here we are."

She turned to the men looking anxious to go. "Okay, this could be our rifle shooter who took out two of our possible informants, and he may be the person who will take the hit on the President day after tomorrow. We don't know if he's even in his room, but we'll go take a look and if not, we'll just wait for him."

Lynn led her troops into the hotel, pulling a hotel security man to the side and told him to find his supervisor and tell him that Metro is in the building to take down a hitman. She said to tell him not make it a big deal, as it was under the radar to catch the man, telling him room 204. Lynn went to the elevators with the troops and then up to the floor of the room. They stood down the hallway as another elevator opened and out came the head of hotel security followed by two of his men in nice suits.

"I'm Adam Ross, head of security. Is this going to be a messy affair?" he asked.

"Hopefully it won't, the hitman doesn't know we are on to him. We just need to get into the room to see if he's here and find out if he's our bad guy."

"Do you have a warrant?"

"Nope, we were hoping to find probable cause to enter the room."

The man stood looking at Lynn, "Is this man really bad?"

"Between you and me, he may be here to assassinate the President on his visit."

"No warrant? For an assassin."

"We aren't really sure it's him, all circumstantial, but the lead is good. Besides, we're playing cowboy here, we can't trust anyone else right now."

"Okay, Hopalong Cassidy, I may have heard that the neighbors were complaining that there was a gun shot in that room, shall I give you probable cause?"

Lynn smiled and thanked him. They went to the door and the security boss pulled his master key card and quietly slid it in the door lock. He turned the doorknob quietly and opened the door for Lynn and her men. They went flying into the room with weapons out front. They found the room empty of people.

They did find a rifle case with a high-powered M40, bolt-action sniper rifle, as Ross reported, "I was a trained sniper myself in the army, in Viet Nam. This is actually an M40A5, first introduced in 2009, based on the Remington 700 rifle. It will do the job to kill the President."

"So we can assume this is not something a hunter would normally bring into Vegas," Lynn said.

"Only if he's hunting humans on the run in the desert. I'd say you have an assassin."

"Okay, Warren I want you to personally take this in for forensics to check the rifling against the bullets we have from Reslo and Won Ho. Do it quickly and quietly," Lynn said.

Ross closed up the case and Warren took the rifle followed by two uniforms and left. "Are you going to wait for this man to come back?" Ross asked.

"If we want to arrest him, we need a crime, but just having this weapon can be grounds for suspicion and we can at least take him in for questioning. It may slow him down for his purpose of assassination until we get the results from forensics on the rifle."

"Glad I could help. Now I have duties to do so you are on your own here. If you need me to state I let you in due to suspicious activities, just call."

"Thanks, We'll lock up after we are finished," Lynn said as Ross went out followed by his men. She turned to us and said, "Dig around to see if we can find anything to associate his guy with Nabib."

We were digging through the suite and found nothing other than tickets from and to New York and guides to Vegas for shows on the desk.

"We may have fouled up the plan to hit the President and if we can keep it under the radar, Nabib may not have time to hire another hitman," I said. "But he still has the bomb," I added.

"Hopefully the Feds can locate that and disarm it. If not, we'd better think about relocating. This reminds me of the attempt of your terrorist with the Area 51 virus. This city is getting dangerous."

I thought that also. This city was full of money and important people, it was a flame for the moths of crime to hit and hit hard. I went to the window and looked out at the strip up to the Stratosphere, still finding a thrill at the sight, even though I still could see the crime and dangerous people who would screw up the beauty. I thought maybe I should go into a safer, less dangerous occupation. Penny would like that.

We waited around the suite and couldn't find any more evidence that this man was part of the attempt to further Nabib's cause for the liberation of his people. Or so he says.

Lynn came over and said, "I want to thank you for your help, I don't say it enough but you do make life easier for us. Thank you."

"You won't thank me after you get my bill," I laughed, "Now what do we do, the Feds are all pawing after Nabib and we probably have his hitman. Effectively stopping the assassination attempt, so Nabib will have to blow up Vegas to prove his point. Are we getting the job done? Or will the Feds be able to find the bomb?"

"I'm still overwhelmed by the magnitude of this whole thing. It's bad enough we had to endure the threat of destruction from your terrorist threatening to wipe out Vegas with a virus, now we have a nut case wanting to spread radiation to destroy our economy and make people really sick. I hope the Feds can do the job. I may not like them but I think we may need to cooperate with them."

"You're not going to call Carlton in on this are you?"

"Oh hell no, I'm calling my training instructor Troy, he's the anti-terrorist expert, he should be able to help and maybe he can go over Carlton's head."

We were standing at the window when we heard the door start to open. Everyone pulled their weapons and waited. The man came into the room and dropped a brief case by the door and looked up to us, startled.

"Hands up DeMolay! Police!" Lynn yelled.

He slowly put his hands in the air, looking to all the guns pointed at him and said quietly, "I guess I don't have much of a choice, do I?"
**

Chapter 28

They had DeMolay in interrogation room six, down away from the squad room, an older, less used interrogation room and safe from the prying eyes of the Feds who invaded the squad room. They brought him in the back way and smuggled him into the station while everyone was busy with their own problems. Lynn went into the room with Deacon, I watched from the observation room with the DA brought in from a call by Lynn, just to cover all bases.

Lynn sat across from DeMolay and waited. The man just sat coolly and calm staring back to Lynn. He finally spoke, "What do you have to detain me, if nothing but conjecture, then I'm walking out of here now."

"Not so fast Stephen, we have the rifle found in your room and Forensic says it matches the slugs taken from two dead men, Dominic Reslo and Won Ho. Now, you are going down for those murders, but our main problem here is greater than your piddly little crime of murdering two scumbags. Maybe you did the world a service. What we want is Fasel Nabib and you can lead us to him."

DeMolay sat straight up and silent. He looked to Deacon and then back to Lynn. "I don't know a Fasel Nabib."

"Are you afraid of him DeMolay, is that what it is. Afraid of this man who is better at killing than you?"

"No one is better at killing than me," he snarled. "You already know I am a killer for hire, so it's pointless to hide the fact. But I don't know this Nabib you talk about."

Lynn looked to Deacon then back to DeMolay, "So you weren't brought in to shoot our beloved Mayor in two days?" Lynn said to trip up the killer. She watched his eyes for a flash of concern over her faux pas.

"I am saying I wasn't brought here to kill your mayor or anyone else other than Reslo and Ho. I was told they were liabilities for the people who hired me."

"Just who were the people who hired you Stephen?"

He flashed a devilish grin and said, "I guess that's for me to know and you to find out."

Lynn looked to Deacon and said, "I guess he's got us over a barrel. Why don't we go out and call in the Homeland Security people along with the FBI all waiting out there and we can turn him over to them. We lowly cops can't torture him into telling, but they can. Go bring in Special Agent Carlton and have him take this scum away."

"Lieutenant, you really want me to give him to Carlton? The man killed the hitman, Spider, in his cell right in FBI headquarters."

DeMolay made a noise and said, "Spider is dead?" These hitmen all knew their competition and DeMolay knew who Spider was.

Lynn turned to him and said, "Yes, he was poisoned in a FBI holding cell. The same cell you are going to go to unless you cooperate." She smiled at him and went silent.

He was now thinking, his eyes searched the two people in front of him for a sign of deceit but found none.

"Look I'm telling you straight, I don't know this Nabib character. I was brought out here to do a hit on Dominic Reslo. While I was here, they asked me to take out some fat oriental at that bar the cops were at. That's all I know, honestly."

"Okay who are these people who hired you?"

"The Vespar family, on orders from Palo Vespar," he said quietly as if he didn't want anyone to hear his confession.

Lynn was briefed earlier on the Vespar family by Deacon and me, she said, "You better be really straight with us, we need to find a shooter as good as you or better in the Vegas area."

He looked like he was thinking and said, "Now that Spider is dead, I'm the best, but there is one other. I trained him a few years ago and I'm sure I saw him in town. He's still not as good as me, but he could do the hit on your Mayor."

"Okay, who is he and where did you see him?"

"I caught a glimpse of him at the Paris Hotel as I was walking down the strip. He didn't see me and I didn't want him to."

"What's his name?"

"Arthur Fraser, he's about thirty and slim, dark hair and a scar down his right cheek. I gave him that while I trained him; he was slow. I don't think he appreciated it."

I was listening to all the talk in the room and thought about the route I saw on the map at Nabib's warehouse. The route took the president's car right in front of the replica Eiffel Tower at the Paris Hotel. I wondered if it could be a place from where this Fraser could shoot the President from. I'd have to mention it to Lynn.

"Okay, DeMolay, we'll check on this. You will be placed in a holding cell until we can figure out the charges for the hit on Reslo and Ho. Have a nice night." She stood followed by Deacon and they went out of the room.

I went out of the observation room with the DA on my heels. We approached Lynn and Deacon as she was on her cell phone. I could hear her requesting a check on an Arthur Fraser staying at the Paris Hotel. She hung up and turned to me, as I told her about my idea of Fraser shooting from the Eiffel Tower.

She snickered, "You think he may shoot the President from the replica French monument?"

"Well the French aren't very friendly people, so yes. Is it a coincidence that Fraser is at the Paris Hotel and the tower is on the route for the motorcade. I just put the numbers together and it came out to one."

The DA spoke, "Your case on DeMolay is good, since we have his prints on the rifle that killed Reslo and Ho, but his statement on Fraser can be construed as circumstantial. So proceed carefully." He finished and went off down the hall and out.

Deacon said, "I still hate lawyers, even if they are on our side."

"Well, what's the plan now?" I asked.

"I'm waiting for Warren to find out if Fraser is staying at the Paris Hotel; I don't want to invade the place if he's not there. We're already in deep by not telling the Feds about DeMolay."

We heard a commotion behind us down the hall and then a uniform came running up to Lynn, talking to her quietly, "Lieutenant, that DeMolay guy overpowered the guard and he got out the back door with a hostage."

"Shit! Who's the hostage?"

"One of the other guards, but DeMolay let him loose in the parking lot, DeMolay is gone."

Lynn looked to us and sighed, "Can anything more go wrong today? Let's get on this Fraser thing before that screws up. I'm not worrying about DeMolay, but you can put out an APB on him for two counts of murder," she said to the officer and he went off.

Warren turned a corner and saw us, he came over. "Lieutenant, it took a bit of finagling, but I got the Paris Hotel to tell me that there's no Arthur Fraser registered at their hotel. He could be under an assumed name, if you have a photo, I can go have them take a look."

"We only have a name and a brief description of him, see if you can pull him up on the LEIN and hopefully they have a photo. He has a big scar on the right side of his face if that helps." Warren said he would check and went off to his desk.

Lynn looked down the long hallway out into the squad room and could see Agent Carlton heading our way. "Crap, here comes Carlton, let's get out of here." We all turned and went out to the back entrance and gathered as far from the building as we could hide.

"This is stupid, having to run from our jobs," she said. Lynn's cell phone rang, she looked at the ID, "More bad news, it's Weber." She answered, "Yes, Captain?"

"Where are you?"

"I'm in the back parking lot, do you need me?"

"Agent Carlton is requesting your presence. Do you have time?"

"No, not really for him, I have a lead on a shooter who may be the assassin. I need to go to the hotel we have word he may be at."

"Where would that be?" Weber said quietly as if Carlton may be near.

"If I tell you, then you'd have to fib. So I don't think I will."

"I got that, Carter. Be careful and I'll stall here." They hung up and Lynn turned back to us.

"Okay troops, we have no other options, so let's go to Paris."

We all piled into our cars and drove over to the strip and around the building that housed the Paris Hotel. We parked the cars and went into the lobby and Lynn took lead on the check-in counter.

"I'm homicide Detective Lieutenant Lynn Carter, may I speak to your supervisor?" she asked of the clerk.

The girl picked up her phone and made a call, then told us the super would be here shortly. We waited and then a tall thin man came up and asked if he could help. Lynn signaled him to step down to the end of the counter.

"We're in pursuit of a possible hitman and assassin, we have fairly good information that he may be staying here. Can you possibly help us?"

"I'll do what I can, do you have a picture?"

"That's the problem, we don't, but he's about thirty and slim, dark hair and a large scar down his right cheek."

I was standing next to them as Lynn was giving the description and then I saw him standing by the show ticket booth. I tapped Lynn on her shoulder and carefully pointed. She turned, seeing what I was pointing to and grinned.

**

Chapter 29

Lynn signaled to Deacon to go around the other side of Fraser and whispered to Trapper and me to stay behind her. We had our weapons out and close to our sides so not to frighten any tourists, causing them to scream and tipping our hand.

Deacon was situated on the other side of the man as Lynn went up to him saying, "Excuse me sir, do you know what the time is?"

Fraser lifted his arm to look at his watch when Lynn brought up her cuffs and flipped one of the bracelets on his wrist. He gave a surprised yell as Deacon grabbed his other wrist bringing it behind him and they slapped the other cuff on him. He was fussing as Lynn pulled her badge and showed him, saying, "Arthur Fraser, you are being detained for suspicion of attempt to commit an assassination." She pointed to Deacon and he gave him the Miranda rights.

He just stared to Lynn now and then said, "You are making a big mistake, Lieutenant."

Lynn froze wondering how the man knew she was a lieutenant. "What's that mean Fraser?"

"Check my jacket pocket. Top right."

Lynn reached in and pulled out a wallet, flipping it open, her heart lost a couple beats, it was a badge of the Secret Service with an ID to match. She looked to him matching the picture and asked, "What the hell is this?"

"You better have a good explanation for this," he said. Lynn and Deacon pulled the man over to the side by the end of the counter near a wall and she asked again, "You are with Secret Service?"

"Yes, as my ID will tell you, I'm a Captain of the President's private security team. I'm here to check out the hotels for unusual activities."

"Do you know a hitman named DeMolay?"

"Stephen DeMolay, how do you know him and where is he?"

Lynn reached around and removed the cuffs, "I don't think you're going to like what I'm about to tell you."

A half hour later, sitting on a bench in the lobby Lynn had detailed the story to Fraser. He actually smiled.

"That's funny. DeMolay and I go back a number of years. I caught him a few times but he always managed to slip out on me, so don't feel about bad your losing him. So he's in town, with his weapons, but you have them now. He can resupply his stock, but for him to be in town is not good."

"How much do you know of the plot to shoot the President and about the bomb?"

"Are you referring to Fasel Nabib?" he said.

Lynn was a bit struck by the comment, "Yes, does the Secret Service know where he is?"

"Sure, he's dead. We found his body yesterday during our investigation. We have been investigating, even though it seems like we aren't."

"Then what are all those people in our precinct doing?"

"Running around with their heads up their asses," he laughed and then, "Is Ross Carlton still heading up the investigation?"

Deacon spoke, "Yes, the ass is."

"He was told yesterday that we had Nabib. He is probably trying to locate the bomb so he's keeping the investigation alive and coming out a hero. He's a douche and almost got busted for giving a suspect a mild poison then withholding the antidote until the suspect confessed."

"Crap, we just lost a suspect to poisoning a couple days ago, while under his care." Deacon chimed in.

"Really? I'll have to talk to someone about that. He hides all his screw-ups real well. I'll see he goes down for that."

"You called me Lieutenant earlier, how did you know?"

"We have dossiers on everyone involved in this investigation, even the LVMPD. I recognized you, but couldn't figure why you were detaining me. Now we are all on the same page. You have any leads as to where the bomb may be?"

"We discovered a lead to a stolen hearse and were told that it may be in a coffin."

Lynn said that and I got a chill again thinking about my dream.

"Interesting, have you tracked the car?"

"We have men watching for the plates, just so we don't pull over every funeral procession."

"Hopefully they didn't change the plates."

Lynn paused, "I wish you hadn't said that."

He laughed again and said, "Just look for a procession with no followers."

Lynn and Deacon laughed together and then Lynn continued, "So you are here to check the hotels?

"Well, we had word that DeMolay was here somewhere, so I was going around with his picture checking. I was showing the picture to the ticket lady when you came up." He pulled the photo from his lower pocket and showed it to Lynn and Deacon.

"Yep, that's him. Do you think he will make an attempt on the President and who is behind his hire?"

"We do suspect he will, and he was hired by the Vespar mob family out of LA."

"Oh yeah, we're aware of them. Why do they want the President dead, probably for many reasons, but what is theirs?"

"Money, lots of it. If they hit the President, it will cause confusion and then with the bomb they can threaten the Vice President into paying them a fortune, transferring it to an offshore account. It will be in the billions. The Vespars are trying to keep their

189

heads low and blaming Afghanistan's branch of the al-Qa'ida, but we know they are behind it. Nabib was brought in to be cover for them but we figure he got a big head to take over so they did a hit on him."

"Why not just go in and bust them?"

"We don't know where the bomb is yet and we aren't taking the chance that these idiots will set the damn thing off. Once we find the bomb we can take them down."

"Well, we are at your disposal, just let us know what we can do."

"You have already given me intel that will be helpful. I can use a bunch of good eyes in this so just continue with what you're doing."

"What about Carlton?" Deacon asked.

"Ignore him, I'll make a few calls and he'll be out of there fast."

"Good," Deacon said with a grin.

We stormed back into the precinct, walking into the squad room and up to Carlton. He gave us a smug look and said, "Well, it's about time you showed up, you left us in the lurch here, I'm not happy."

Deacon said to Lynn, "Let me take this." He got into Carlton's face and said, "Carlton, go screw yourself."

"I said this before, don't screw with me. I'll have your badge!" He heard a voice behind him and turned to see the Director of the Las Vegas FBI standing there.

"Carlton, you are being relieved of your duties, and these two agents will take you in for questioning on the murder of Horace Worley, AKA Spider. Turn over your weapon and shield."

Carlton looked shocked. He slowly reached for his weapon and removed it, handing it to the Director along with his badge wallet. He held his head down as he was taken out followed by the Director.

"Now we can get some investigating done," Deacon said.

Weber came up after watching the drama unfold. "Okay, what do you have?"

Lynn and Deacon spent the next half hour in his office going over everything they had. They came out and over to Trapper and me sitting at Warren's desk. Warren had been listening to us relate the events of the day and enjoying the put down of Carlton, he didn't like him either.

"Weber has given us full authority to go find the bomb and DeMolay. The feds are cooperating by conducting their own investigation, but we are swapping intel as we receive it. Fraser said their last communication in regards to DeMolay had him at the Monte Carlo again. We didn't leave anyone at his room and he went in to clean out of all his personal items. He left the hotel without paying and they weren't happy and called the police."

"So we still have no idea where he may be?" I said.

"Nope, think your little buddies in the mob may know?" she said with a smirk.

"I can call and see if their network can track him down, but time is fleeting. I'm also wearing down and would like to go see my family. I'll call Angelo from home after I give my wife a big kiss." I saluted and walked out followed by Trapper since I was his ride. We got back to the office and it was closed, everyone had left. I dropped Trapper at his car and then I drove home.

I arrived at the house, parked in the garage and found my lovely wife and faithful dog swimming in the pool. I stripped down quickly to my BVD's and jumped in surprising Penny. When I came up for air she asked, "Are you changing your ways now. Am I going to enjoy your company swimming with me?"

"I just wanted to wash off the insanity of the day. I am glad to be home and I may take up a new occupation. Wouldn't you like that?"

"No, because you'd be miserable, and then you'd make me miserable and then make Willy miserable. So don't even threaten us with giving up. Besides Las Vegas needs you to protect them from all the bad guys.

I swam on my back thinking about the bad guys. Then took a big breath and went underwater to come up in front of Penny with a big wet kiss.

*

Chapter 30

Early the next morning we awoke to the phone ringing. I checked the caller ID and it said private, I hated those calls, but answered. It was Angelo.

"Hey guy, what did you find?" I asked.

"Well, Mr. R. it seems that DeMolay is moving around a lot. My union sources in the hotels have been keeping track of him for you. Call the Mirage Hotel and ask for housekeeping, talk to Nestor Dimucci, he's an old friend. He has the inside on DeMolay's activities; he'll help you follow the scum. As for the Vespar family, they have a small bunch of wiseguys in town, staying at a local bed and breakfast owned by the Vespar family, name's something like 'A Touch of Sicily'. Look it up, you'll find it. They have a really big garage in back I'm told, it may have your missing hearse."

"Thank you again, my friend, the United States owes you a debt of gratitude for helping to protect the President. I'll talk later." We finished and hung up. I noticed that Angelo's speech was improving, he must be taking lessons. I rolled over and kissed Penny still prone on the bed.

She turned her head to me to accept the kiss and said, "Off to save the world now?"

"Yep, where's my mask and cape?"

"We've been through this before, I told you, over next to your pink tights," she giggled and kissed my nose.

I was up and finished in the bathroom, as Penny was getting ready to go to her station to interview famous celebrities. Willy was all ready to go with her and waited by the door. The two of them went off and I stood looking out the front window at the sight of the Vegas strip shining in the morning sun just coming over the mountains.

I gathered all my props to fight crime and went to the car, driving out and over to Metro. I parked in the back lot and went in to find less people in the squad room. I saw Warren at his desk and asked what happened to everyone.

"Well, since Carlton was ousted, they all sort of went off to do some real investigating. Lynn and Deacon are in Weber's office getting the poop on the Secret Service's latest info. They should be done soon."

I thanked him, went to Lynn's office and sat. I was playing solitaire on my Palm TX when Lynn and Deacon breezed into the office.

"Why don't you just make yourself to home," Lynn said with a smile.

"I got some info for you," I said and told them what Angelo told me. Lynn reached for her local phone book and looked up the B&B. She found it and said, "This is good." She yelled out to Warren and said to get some men together and they were going to chase the Vespar family. Warren's eyes went big and he smiled. He went off and Lynn looked back to me, "Maybe we can find the bomb, but we still need to stop DeMolay. I really want to roast his balls when I get him for lying to me. I felt like an idiot arresting Fraser. I'll go talk to Weber about a warrant and then we can go."

About an hour later the warrant had come in and so did the Secret Service, led by Fraser. "You didn't think I would let you have all the fun did you?" he said with a grin.

"How'd you find out so fast?" Deacon asked.

"I made Captain Weber swear to an oath to let me know any new developments. So here I am."

"It's fine with me, do you have anyone experienced with nuclear devices?" Lynn asked.

"I have a team standing by provided by the FBI, they felt bad about subjecting us to Carlton."

"Okay, we have all we need then, let's roll out," Lynn said as she led the charge. Between our cars, four patrol cars, the SWAT van and the Secret Service attack team, we made a pretty sight rolling up Vegas Boulevard with flashers and sirens going. Must have scared the tourists, as we ran through lights, then arrived up off Sahara and down Decatur to the large building housing the mob infested B&B. The LVMPD uniforms wearing riot gear surrounded the building and Lynn, Deacon, Fraser and most of the SWAT team went to the large garage and busted the door open.

The rest of the police had formed a wall of guns between the main house and the garage to stop intrusions from the mob. We entered the garage and found the hearse, Lynn checked the plates and it was the stolen one from Spenser Funeral Home. Fraser opened the back door to the hearse and let the bomb tech's get at the coffin still in the car. They slid out the tray holding the coffin and carefully opened it. The bomb was there.

From in the garage, we started hearing gunfire and carefully went to the door and looked out. The outside police officers were scattering and firing back at the house. The idiot wiseguys thought they could out shoot cops, SWAT and Feds. I noticed that the coffin was exposed to the open overhead door and bullets were hitting dangerously close to the box. I had heart palpations watching the box being hit by fire and I signaled to Fraser and pointed.

"They're going to hit the thing!" I yelled. Fraser reached up and pulled on the rope for the overhead door causing it to come down. The bomb techs were scrambling to get the bomb out of the coffin and into a thick lead box they brought in especially for this type of weapon. They had it in and locked the lid.

The gunfire had ceased and I looked out the window and saw the police holding a number of men in the parking lot. The wiseguys probably figured they were outnumbered and surrendered, better to fight in court than be killed.

Fraser ran the overhead door back up and the bomb techs rushed the device to a waiting step van and drove off with it. Fraser went to a man who was being identified as the leader of the group.

"You're Dickie Salvatore, I've seen your mug shots. Must say you look better in the pictures. Now tell me where DeMolay is."

"Screw you cop. DeMolay will still carry out the attack on the President. We will at least have our day."

Fraser told the Vegas officers to take the men in to holding for transfer to the federal building for jailing. He turned to us, "Thanks for your help."

I laughed and told him that I had a friend in the Traviano mob family out in New York who gave us the tip to find this place.

"Well, that's a new one, give our thanks to your friend. Now we need DeMolay. Do your contacts know where he may be?"

"I have some inside help on that. I called a local source and they say he was last in the Mirage Hotel," I said.

Fraser looked to Lynn and said, "Shall we go there?"

"Lead the way," she said.

I followed them out to their cars, running into Trapper coming up to the lot. He stopped and asked if he missed anything. I opened his car door and got in waving to Lynn, saying I was driving with Will. I told him where we were going and he drove that way.

"How did you find us?"

"I still have contacts in the precinct, they told me where you guys went. So what's up?"

"We got the bomb and now we have to find DeMolay. I called a contact in the hotel union and they say he's in the Mirage."

"Great, we can go see some lions and then catch a hitman," Trapper said referring to the lions on display from the former Siegfried and Roy magic shows that played the Mirage before one of the cats attacked Roy, putting him on the disabled list.

We arrived at the Mirage and Trapper parked behind Lynn's unmarked car, then we went in. I had called Dimucci on the way over and he said his people had been quietly watching DeMolay and he was still in his room. He said it was 406.

Once again the tourists were treated to an army of cops, SWAT and feds walking through the hotel lobby. Hotel security approached our troops and asked what we were up to, Lynn informed them and they led us to the elevators and up to the floor.

197

Mortuary Murders

As we came out of the elevator Lynn eyes met with DeMolay's as he came of his room. His eyes went big as he remembered Lynn from the precinct and he spun to go back down the hallway towards the stairwell. Hotel security called on their phone to follow the man with the cameras. He listened as they reported DeMolay's journey. Lynn and her crew had already ran after DeMolay and were barreling down the stairwell after listening for his footfalls.

DeMolay burst out from the lower stairwell to the lobby, then over to the casino floor and was lost in the crowd as Lynn and our team came out. We ran through the casino floor as we spread out. I was by the blackjack tables and saw DeMolay sitting at one table, I watched him trying to hide his face then I saw Lynn skulking around the crowd and I waved to her. As she came over, DeMolay saw us and burst away from the table and over to the slot machines.

He ran down the aisles of people playing slots and knocked over a few gray haired ladies pumping coins into the machines. One uniformed security guard saw DeMolay disrupting the tourists and tried to stop him not knowing who he was. DeMolay gave him an openhanded crack to the his throat and he went down. I came by the guard and he was hurt, but all right. Lynn sped by me in pursuit along with Deacon and Fraser. The rest of the team had spread out on the casino floor and were trying to corner the man, but he put up a good fight.

He was closing in on the front open doors but saw that he was blocked by uniforms at the entrance. He turned to the right, found a door on the side of the casino floor and entered. There was a short hallway and another door that was raised up off the ground. The sign on the door said 'Do Not Enter', after breaking the lock, he went in. After he was in the door, he came out into what looked like a wildlife habitat, he moved around the fake rocks and turned to see two very large lions resting on the upper rocks. They saw him and came down quickly. The lions were once part of the Siegfried and Roy magic show and were fairly tame, but DeMolay didn't know this. He panicked as the cats approached and he took out a gun, pointed it at the lead cat and was just about to fire when a third lion hit him from behind.

*

Chapter 31

Men, women and children were all screaming as they watched from outside the thick reinforced glass wall that kept the lions from attacking tourists. Lynn, Deacon, Trapper, Fraser and I came running into the lobby where the glass enclosures were and saw DeMolay on the floor with the big cat on top of him, more playing than hurting.

DeMolay was so frightened that he forgot about the gun, then realized he had it, fired it but only hit the ceiling as the lion clamped down on his arm. The shot had frightened the two other cats and they ran to a neutral corner of the enclosure.

Mortuary Murders

"We better get him out of there before he hurts a lion," Lynn said and then we ran from the lobby around to the doorway where the entrance to the enclosure was. By this time, the animal handlers were aware of the incident hearing the gun shot and were scrambling to get in and subdue the beast.

About thirty minutes later, the lions were returned to their pens and DeMolay was carried out on a stretcher by EMS followed by the Secret Service agents. He was badly shaken and had a couple broken bones but was relatively unharmed. Hotel security had the sightseers all moved out of the area and I stood watching the whole circus being performed to my delight.

I had no more to contribute, the bomb was captured and DeMolay wasn't going to threaten the President, the mob wiseguys were all rounded up, so I decided to call it a day and go see what my office looked like. I hadn't been in it much lately and I was sure Penny would be coming in soon. I went to Lynn, "You have the situation well in hand, I'm going to where it's safer. See you guys later." I left the Mirage along with Trapper, who drove me there.

"Well, it's all over now, are you happy?" Trapper asked as we rode out Tropicana to Metro PD.

I looked at him thinking it was a strange thing to say, "Happy? I'm always happy when we stop a crime from happening. I wouldn't say happy… I'd say more satisfied. Tomorrow the President will drive up Las Vegas Boulevard not even knowing that he was marked for death and the city is safe from being a vast radioactive wasteland, yeah I guess I can say I'm happy now. By the way how did your trip to Denver go?"

He laughed, "Not really exciting, we were involved in a double murder and caught a long thought dead serial killer who was living in his mother's basement. Other than that, it was all normal. Phil is now Phyllis and Sam is in a good place with it. We have to go back in a week or so to bring Phyllis back and we'll introduce you."

"Thanks, I look forward to it." I sat watching the scenery going by as Trapper drove me back to Metro to get my car. I waved him off as he drove away and I climbed into my Crown Vic and sat for a minute. I pulled my cell phone and called Penny. "Where are you?" I asked when she came on.

"I'm in your office playing Mah Jong on your computer, are you coming in?" she asked.

"I'm on my way; shall we go eat at Bistros?"

"Good idea, I could use some good food."

"I'll be there in a couple minutes watch for me."

We had a nice lunch at Bistros and I told Penny all about my day and the chase of DeMolay. I said I'd have to call Angelo and let him know he was invaluable for his help. We left Bistros and went back to the office, Lacey smiled as we came in the front door. Buck was standing at the counter talking to a couple men who I presumed were new guards. Buck waved to us and took the men to his office.

"Well, how was your adventure saving the President?" Lacey asked. "Trapper came in and told me about DeMolay in the lion's den, there's a parable in there somewhere. And we had a woman come in earlier about her husband being murdered; I told her you'd call her."

"I think I'll wait on that. I need to relax a bit first before I get involved in another murder."

"Well, she said she thinks he was killed by a crazy hypnotist who has a show at Fitzgerald's, it sounded interesting."

"Yes it does, but later, now I'm taking Penny and going into my office and closing the door, don't disturb us since we will be necking." I smiled and took Penny by the hand and pulled her down the hallway.

We were up early the next morning; it was Saturday so Penny didn't have to work. We sat in front of the Jumbo LCD TV on the living room wall watching the ceremony at the county building for the President. The mayor was in his glory for the photo op and the city council were all gathered around trying to look important. I wasn't a political person, I had no interest in the people who ran the country for their short terms, if they screwed things up, then next administration would come in and make a bigger mess or maybe even fix a few broken things.

I had called Angelo last night and relayed the story and he was pleased. Penny was also pleased that the case was over, she told me she always worries when I go out on a crime. The phone rang as we rested on the couch, I reached over to the end table and took the receiver off the base and answered. It was Deacon.

"Hey, what's happening?" I asked

"Just thought you'd like to know, DeMolay is tucked away in Federal prison for trial and the bomb has gone out to Nellis Air Base for transport to wherever they keep nuclear bombs. The Vespar family is going to be under indictment for the plot to do harm to Vegas and the President, so all is well. How are you doing this morning?"

"Alive and well. Penny and I are just going to vegetate here today, maybe get some swim time in." Penny gave me a big smile when I said that. "You know, you and Lynn should go away together for a couple days to recharge your batteries and get in a lot of sex."

I could hear him laugh, "Where do you think we are right now?"

"I have no idea but I'm getting a mental image, does it involve a motel and handcuffs?"

I heard him laugh really hard and he just said, "Later." Then he hung up.

**

THE END
For every ending, there's a new beginning.

Now read a preview of
Hypnotic Murders by Bob Moats

Chapter 1

The man in the tuxedo cautiously walked through Casino Royale in search of Le Chiffre. He came to the Baccarat table where he saw Vesper sitting with cards in front of her. The tuxedo man stood for a moment when one of the bodyguards for Le Chiffre turned to him and pulled a weapon. The tuxedo man pulled his Walter PPK and fired on the man, hitting him in the chest three times dead center. Men in security uniforms came rushing up with weapons drawn and yelled for the tuxedo man to drop his weapon. He didn't, and raised the weapon to protect himself as the guards all fired on the man, killing him.

Las Vegas Metro PD homicide Detective Lynn Carter and Sergeant Frank DeAngelo, AKA Deacon, had arrived about thirty minutes later to find the body covered with a sheet and the gawkers were held back by the crime scene yellow tape. The hotel security at the Rio Hotel and Casino were busy keeping tourists from being in the area, but it was difficult as it was now a place of interest.

Lynn bent down to the body, lifting the sheet and then looked to Joe Lang, County coroner, and asked, "Who is he, Joe?"

"Name's Mike Finch, business cards in his wallet says had a stock brokerage over in Summerlin. They say he strolled in and pulled a twenty-two and started firing. He hit three people, luckily, no one was killed, and then security had to put him down when he refused to stop. They say he looked like he was drugged, but I'll know better when I get him back to the morgue and dig into him."

"Thanks Joe, another meth head gone bad probably." Lynn said as she stood, looking down at the man in jeans and blue dress shirt.

The next day I was in my office when the

woman came in the front entrance ringing the small bell on the door making its tinkling noise. I sat waiting for Lacey, my office manager and receptionist to let me know what I had in store.

She came to my private office door and said there was a woman wanting help. I stood and went out to find an attractive blond, about five-six and well built standing at the counter.

"Hi there, I'm Jim Richards, how may I help you." I was careful how I worded things since she was a looker and I didn't want my wife to misconstrue my intentions. My beautiful Las Vegas TV talk show host and wife, Penny Wickens-Richards had this telepathy thing about her that could tell if I was unfaithful even in my mind, so I was always cautious about my wording.

"I'm Celeste Finch and my husband was murdered and I want you to bring the killer to justice. I know who the killer is and you have to prove he did it."

"Okay, please follow me to my office and we'll talk." I winked at Lacey as she sat at her desk and took the widow to my office. I motioned her to the client chair as I sat at my desk.

"You say you know who your husband's killer was? Have you told the police?"

"Yes, I told this Detective Carter, but I think she thought I was crazy. I need someone to investigate and not make fun of my suspicions.

"Okay, I personally know Detective Carter, and she is a fair and dedicated homicide officer, but sometimes things don't always add up for the police.

You may have some important information that may help me to solve your case, information that the police may not look into. Can you tell me more about what happened?"

"Three nights ago my husband, Mike, and I took some business clients to the Fitzgerald Hotel to see this hypnotist and the man called my husband to the stage to help. He hypnotized my husband and told him he was James Bond and had him act out a few things that Bond would do, stand like him and tell the audience that he was agent 007. Yesterday my husband left our home then went to the Rio Hotel and into the casino where he shot three people before the security shot him dead. I don't blame the guards, I say the hypnotist had him commit the attack that resulted in his death. The police said they'd look into it, but I think they were just blowing me off."

"Well, I'll have a talk with Detective Carter and see what they have done on this. Do you want me to investigate?"

"Yes, Mr. Richards, I hear you are a good detective yourself and help people. Please clear my husband's name and take down this man."

"I'll see what I can do. What did your husband do for a living?"

"He was an investment broker, handled lots of money transactions for his clients, one of whom we took to the show that night."

"I see, do you think the death of your husband was in connection to his business?"

"I don't know; he never spoke to me about his business. If there was any money stolen or transferred because of this, I wouldn't know."

"Okay, please write down everything I need to know, names and places, times of the incidents, and where I can reach you." I pushed my pad of paper and a pen to her as I caught a glimpse of her ample breasts in the low cut blouse; I was going to catch hell for that later.

She spent about ten minutes writing and then pushed the pad and pen back to me. "Thank you, this is my rate card, will you be able to pay for my services? I'm not trying to be rude, but some people who come here aren't very well off and still I try to help them." She looked to the card I handed her with my rates and then took out her wallet from her purse and removed four hundred dollars in large bills and put them on my desk. "Money's no problem for me, here's the retainer. Mr. Richards, please take this killer down for me."

"I'll do my best." We stood and she went out of my office as I followed her to the lobby, getting a good look at her caboose. Well-rounded, oh hell, I was going to suffer for that too, when I got home.

She turned, smiled and said, "It's a pleasure to meet you, I've read a good number of articles in the Review-Journal about your exploits. I know I can trust you to catch my husband's killer."

"I'll keep you informed, thank you for trusting me with this." She took my hand and we shook, her hand was very soft and warm, giving me thoughts, another reason I was doomed when I got home.

She left and I turned to Lacey, she said with a smile, "I know what you were thinking,".

"Well, stop it. I'm not going there and I'll be dead if I did." I went back to my office and sat trying to think of things that were not sexy, like old fat women in spandex and gray hair. That did it.

I got home around five o'clock and Penny was busy making some good smelling dish. "I didn't stop by today at the office because I had a couple of famous Las Vegas Chefs on my show today and I wanted to try out a couple of dishes they showed me to whip up."

"Well, it smells delicious. What's it called?"

"I can't remember, something Italian, but I remembered the ingredients. So go clean up and get ready for a great meal."

I turned to go to my personal bathroom, it was nice that we each had our own, and I was being followed by our toy Yorkie, Willy. He came into my bathroom with me and I set him on the closed toilet so he could watch as I washed and shaved around my beard. I washed my face and the top of my baldhead and thought about getting some of those hair transplants to fill out my empty space on top. But it would ruin my charming looks, sort of a favorite grandfather type, who everyone trusts and loves. I finished and picked up Willy and we went back out to the dining area where Penny had set out a great spread complete with the good silverware. I sat at my spot as Penny put the hot dishes on the table and then sat.

"How was your day and did you chase after any good looking women?" she asked.

I was in trouble. I'm not very good at telling

Penny tall tales and so I just fessed up, "I had a very attractive woman in today looking for me to catch her husband's killer. Yes, I did look but that was all."

"Good boy, now enjoy your food," was all she said, I was spared the inquisition. We ate and it was very good, a first for my wife.

We finished and I helped clean the table as Penny put the dishes in the dishwasher and we retired to the living room with our beer and chips. We were watching the big screen TV when the driveway alarm went off. I went to the small TV monitor, scanned the area, and saw nothing but a dark colored sedan. The person who had driven it must have gotten out quickly and came to the door. The bell rang and I had my hand on my Glock as I went to the door, opening it, and stared at the visitor. It was our favorite mob wiseguy, Angelo.
**

Continued in the book...

~~*~~

Jim Richards Family of Readers

Thanks to the following people who are now part of the Jim Richards Family of Readers. They have read a book or more and enjoyed them. They all volunteered to be included in the list. If you are a fan of the books, send me your full name and you will be included in future books. Send your name to murdernovels@bobmoats.com to be added here and on the website.

* Achim Feifel * Al Norris * Alex Wheatley * Alexandra Delporte-Wilkinson * Amy Tapia * Andrea Bryan * Anne Shepherd * Arianda Sugar * Arlene Markowski * Ashley Augustus * Audra Hall * Barbara Hughes * Barbara Sammons * Barbara Schuler * Barbara Zirger * Beth Donohue Plenskofski * Betsy Childress * Beth Gibson * Bill Sandy * Bill Tornquist * Billie-jo Collie * Boni J Rychener * Carl Bishopric * Carla Lewis * Carole Henderson * Carolyn Conroy * Carolyn Riddle-Linington * Cassy Bailey * Cathie Turner * Chad Hudson * Charlotte L Duran * Cheryl L. Everett * Cindy Ackley Nunn * Cindy Valstad * Connie Bancroft * Corinne Kay O'Daniel * Dana Robbins Chuchran * Dana Wichita * Danielle Monique * Darren Heald * Dave Travers * David Wilkinson * DeAnn Jannereth * Deanna Miller * Deb Breuker Balbo * Debbie Carter * Debbie White * Deborah Fartuch * Deborah Gauze * Deborah Sullivan * Dee King * Denise Freeman * Diana Carver * Dixie Beck * Donna Gould * Donna Thompson * Donny Minter * Doris Kight

Bob Moats

* Eddie Moore * Eric Walters * Felicia Annette Bradfield * Francine Menor * Gail Chesney * Georgiann Minster * George Conner * Greg Colucci * Hayley Rankin * Harold Garcia * Heidi Arnold * Irma Ranee Coy * Jacqueline Moss * Jan Kimball * Janice Schneider * Janice Spoor * Jennifer Redmond * Jessica Keown-Belous * Jim Beck * Jo Boguslaw * Jo Turner * Joanne Marie Turner * John Peiffer * John Wisbiski * Joseph Wauro * Joyce Stacy * Joyce Trifiletti * Judy Franklin * Judy Travers * Judy Padgett * Julie Heath * Junnahvee Benson * Karen Dahl * Karen Grams * Karen Higham * Karen Kaiser * Karen Meinburg Richwine * Karen Kirkman Parker * Karin Hawkins * Karin Vasvari * Kathleen Donohue Roesing * Kathleen Riddle-Wolfe * Kathy Hinds Moore * Kathy Jones * Kathy Mitchell * Katie Benzler * Kay Burns * Kelly Garcia * Ken Boggs * Keota Rodriguez * Kiera Mccarthy * Kim Estes * Kitty Stolle * Kristie Sciler * Kirsty Stanton * LaLonnie Scallen * Larry Morris * Leann Parr * Lenora Scales * Leslie Marie Jackson * Linda Forester * Linda Ingle Cox * Linda Kennerö * Linda Magill * Lisa Bower * Liz Gibson * Lorraine Wiman * Loretta Alexander * Lynda Bowles * Lynette Lawrance * LuAnn Louttit * Manny Rothman * Marcia Gibson DeWitt * Marie Calder * Marlene Bryan * MaryLouise Kramp * Mary Lynn Gross * Megan Atkins * Meghan Hyden * Melody Cannavan * Michael Carruthers * Michael Dinkens * Michael Vannoy * Michelle Burns-Mitchell * Michelle Pilcher * Micki Potter * Mike Moats * Mimi Baur * Myrna Hecht * Nadine Sutton * Nancy Ellen Sayre * Natalie Quine * Neena Martin * O'Della Wilson * Pat Pollington * Pat Rohn * Patricia Jarmon * Patricia C Trezza * Patrick Barry * Paul Lawrance * Peggy Davis * Phyllis Bassett * Raylene Matheny * Rebecca Collins Besner * Renee Brumley * Reta Hanna * Reta Moats * Roberta Navarro-Harder * Sally Berneathy *

Mortuary Murders

Sally Hubler * Sarah Santos * Satka Nikc * Sharon E. Edwards * Sharon Mangini * Sharon McMillon * Sheena Rawl * Sherry Amstutz * Shirley Alvarez * Shirley Davies * Shirley Williams * Stacie Rowe * Stephanie Conner * Steve Cullen * Susan Haughton * Susan Hesse Adams * Susan Salomon * Suzan K Chase * Taisha Cullum * Tamara Moore * Tammy Castleberry * Tammy Lynn Wood * Ted Murphy * Terri Atkins * Terri Creech * Terry Raab * Tonia Rachael Riggs-Williams * Travis Fleury-Lopez * Twyla Gawlas * Val Brooks * Walt Munsel * Yvonne Isakson *

Thank you to all these wonderful people.

Thank you for purchasing this book. I hope you enjoy it as much as I enjoyed writing it for my faithful readers. Please feel free to email me to tell me what you thought about my stories. I love hearing from the readers. I can be reached at murdernovels@bobmoats.com thanks again!